LUCY GREENHILL
An Utterly Unsuitable Lady

BOOKS

Vinci Books

vinci-books.com

Published by Vinci Books Ltd in 2026

1

Copyright © Lucy Greenhill 2023

The author has asserted their moral right to be identified as the author of this work in accordance with the Copyright, Designs and Patents Act 1988. This work is a work of fiction. Names, characters, places and incidents are the product of the author's imagination or are used fictitiously. Any resemblance to actual persons, living or dead, places and incidents is entirely coincidental.
All rights reserved. No part of this publication may be copied, reproduced, distributed, stored in any retrieval system, or transmitted in any form or by any means, including photocopying, recording, or other electronic or mechanical methods, nor used as a source for any form of machine learning including AI datasets, without the prior written permission of the publisher.
The publisher and the author have made every effort to obtain permissions for any third party material used in this book and to comply with copyright law. Any queries in this respect should be brought to the attention of the publisher and any omissions will be corrected in future editions.
A CIP catalogue record for this book is available from the British Library.
Paperback ISBN: 9781036706029
The EU GPSR authorised representative is Logos Europe, 9 rue Nicolas Poussion, 17000 La Rochelle, France
contact@logoseurope.eu

By Lucy Greenhill

The Moth Agency Romances
An Utterly Unsuitable Lady
A Match for Miss Marshall
The Diva's Daughter

More from Lucy Greenhill writing as Fran Smith

Vita Carew Mysteries
Poison at Pemberton Hall
A Thin Sharp Blade
Dr Potter's Private Practice
The Painted Penny Stamp
The Killing at Crowswood Castle

Chapter One

'I wrote a story at school today,' the boy said. 'Would you like to hear it?'

He and Ida were at the kitchen table shelling peas for supper. The little house was shady, but the sunshine of the summer's evening was still bright outside.

'Yes, of course,' Ida said.

'Perhaps Grandpapa would like to hear it too? Shall I wait?'

They looked out of the back window. A white bearded man in his shirtsleeves was bending over the vegetable patch at the end of the narrow garden.

'Grandpapa can hear it later. Maybe at bedtime.'

The boy fetched an exercise book and climbed back onto his chair, sitting straight-backed and settling himself for a performance. '*Once, in the verdant waters of a tiny stream,*' he began.

'*Verdant waters.* That's very good,' Ida said.

'*... in the verdant waters of a tiny stream,*' the boy repeated,

1

'there lived a silvery minnow. When sunbeams pierced the water, he sparkled and shone and danced among the waving waterweeds.'

'Oh, Oliver! Did you truly write all that yourself?'

'Miss Hurst helped, but I chose the words myself and did most of the spelling.'

'Miss Hurst? Is that a new teacher at the summer school? You have not mentioned her before.'

'She is a helper. I like her. She said it was a promising story.'

'Miss Hurst is right! Is there more?'

'Not yet. I'll probably write some more tomorrow.'

'It is a beautiful story so far. Very beautiful. I could just imagine that little fish in his… '

But the boy was frowning and looking over Ida's shoulder towards the street.

'Ida. Who is that man?'

A knock came at the front door.

Ida and the boy froze and waited. The knock repeated fiercely enough to make the door jump in its frame.

'Cupboard, Ollie,' Ida said.

Taking his exercise book, the boy stepped hurriedly into a tall cupboard in the corner of the kitchen and closed the door behind him.

Summer is a peculiar season in a university city. Examinations over, students have cheerfully fled for vacations. Academics have packed their summer reading into trunks and left for field trips and explorations. The city is left to tourists and residents whose businesses depend upon the passing summer trade.

1894 was a warm, dry summer. College lawns faded to

brown under the sun's glare. Shops kept their awnings over their window displays. The city streets were quiet, as visitors preferred the river, making punting trips to Grantchester or rowing downriver for picnics on Ditton Meadows.

Lucia Venables did not plan a vacation. The Moth Agency–M.O.T.H. standing for Matters of the Heart–was too new to close for the summer. There was rent to pay and clients were few. The population of Cambridge preferred to put its romantic worries behind it and enjoy the sunshine, which meant that she had plenty of time, as this morning, to dust and tidy her small first floor office in Paradise Place.

She straightened the curtains and the floor rug and set a small sprig of lavender in a vase on her desk. She reordered the row of books on her single shelf. She settled the second hand blotter and inkstand in exactly the correct positions. Needing water for the lavender, and–with luck–to offer as refreshment to overheated clients, she took her jug down to the tap in the basement kitchen.

The chances of reaching the kitchen without attracting the attention of Miss Peach, her landlady, were thin. Miss Peach was elderly, but she was spry, with hearing sharp enough never to miss a footstep on the stairs.

'Ah, Miss Venables, good morning,' she said, appearing in the kitchen in her pale summer outfit of lacy white blouse and cream skirt. 'Come to fetch water on a hot day, I see.'

Miss Peach was a great one for stating the obvious.

'Yes, indeed. Good morning, Miss Peach,' her tenant replied. 'I hope you are well this morning.'

'Oh, very well, thank you. We are very well indeed, aren't we, Blossom?'

Mrs Peach's cat and beloved companion was an oversized marmalade creature whose days were spent asleep in the house or murdering the songbird population in the leafy gardens of Paradise Place. He seemed to be asleep on the windowsill, but one ear and the tip of his tail twitched slightly.

Lucia turned off the tap and lifted the jug.

'And do you expect clients this morning?' asked Miss Peach, brightly.

'No appointments so far today, no,' Lucia said.

'Oh dear. None today either. And the rent is due in... let me see... in only three days' time.' Miss Peach smiled and smiled over her silvery spectacles.

The sound of the doorbell interrupted. Miss Peach bustled out to answer it.

'What do you think, Blossom?' Lucia asked the cat. 'Am I in luck?'

The tip of the cat's tail hooked briefly and then fell back. He wasn't committing to an opinion yet.

By the time Lucia arrived, a large lady was already sitting fanning herself in the office. She was red in the face and gasping from the exertion of the stairs, and took several minutes to recover her powers of speech. This gave Lucia time both to pour her a glass of water and to take in her appearance.

She wore widow's black from bonnet to boots, her gown full and elaborate, her hat frilled, beribboned and decorated with several long dark feathers, the tips of which skittered and bobbed with every breath. The lady grasped the glass and swallowed the water in a single draught, then pressed her hand to her heart and fixed Lucia with a fearsome look.

'You are the Miss Venables mentioned on the plate outside?'

'I am. Lucia Venables. How do you do?'

'How do you do?' the lady replied. 'You are younger than one assumed.'

Lucia had no answer for this, so she waited, passing the time by opening her desk drawer and taking out her notebook and pen.

The lady glanced about the room and seemed to reach a conclusion. 'I have need of your services. It says discreet inquiries on your plaque. I should like you to undertake a commission on my behalf,' she said, adding 'discreetly,' as an afterthought.

Lucia wrote the heading 'inquiry' in her notebook using her finest handwriting before asking the lady for a little more information.

The lady sighed deeply and fidgeted with her fan. 'It concerns my son. He is…' she did not end the sentence, but flicked her lacy black fan open and closed several times before saying, 'May I speak in confidence?'

'Absolutely,' Lucia told her.

'My son is—a *professor*,' the lady announced.

'I see,' said Lucia.

'My late husband was also a professor,' the lady added. 'I was widowed many years ago. Professor Watt, Earnest Watt, perhaps you know of him?'

'I'm afraid not.'

The lady did not seem surprised. 'No. He was a philologist. They are a small brotherhood, the philologists, even in academic circles.'

Lucia determined to look the word up in the dictionary at the earliest opportunity.

'My son, on the other hand, went into the natural sciences.'

'Ah,' Lucia said, encouragingly.

'He is very highly regarded in his field. His publications are influential in many quarters. He was made a professor in his thirties. A rare distinction.'

'You must be very proud,' Lucia said.

'Yes, indeed.' The lady nodded. 'I haven't mentioned my own name. It is Dorothea Watt. I am usually known as Mrs Professor Watt.

Lucia nodded. 'And how may I help you, Mrs Watt?'

'Mrs *Professor* Watt, if you don't mind.'

The lady drew herself up for a moment, but then suddenly deflated and sagged back into her chair. 'Oh, Miss Venables, I am at my wits' end. I need someone I can confide in. Please call me...' It took an effort to say this, 'Please call me Mrs Watt, if you find it easier!'

This daring decision seemed to enliven the lady. She sat upright again, set her fan on the desk, and squared her shoulders. 'I need your help urgently. It is a delicate matter... '

Lucia added 'delicate' to the list of words she had written so far.

'My son is a single man. He lives in his college as a bachelor—as do all the Fellows of his college. It suits them. They work in their rooms or in the library, the laboratories or the lecture halls, and they return to college for luncheon and dinner. The food is excellent. The wines carefully chosen. Their rooms are cleaned—in short, they are cared for in every way.'

'So I understand,' Lucia said.

'It is a catastrophe!' declared Mrs Watt.

'Is it?' Lucia asked, surprised.

'As far as their social relationships are concerned, it certainly is. Unless they make great efforts, they never meet an eligible young woman.'

'But many of them do marry, in point of fact,' Lucia remarked.

'Only if they are persuaded out of their work for long enough to find someone suitable, which my son never can be.'

'Perhaps he is simply not inclined to marry.'

Lucia offered the thought mildly enough, but the lady was having none of it.

'How would he even know whether he is inclined or not? He never looks up from his fish long enough to give the matter a single thought!'

'Fish?'

'He is an ichthyologist. An expert on fish. Prehistorical fish fossils—he is a leading authority,' Mrs Watt said, sounding exasperated.

'And what sort of assistance might I be able to offer in this matter, Mrs Watt?'

'You can help me find him a wife,' the lady declared. 'I have run myself ragged for several years attempting to do so. I have introduced him to numerous charming, intelligent and even handsome young women, but I simply cannot keep him away from his work long enough for them to… to…'

'… to become better acquainted?' Lucia suggested.

'To fall in love; to become engaged; to marry! I long for grandchildren, Miss Venables! Call me a selfish old woman…' Mrs Watt struggled through her pockets for a handkerchief, pulled one out and dabbed her eyes. '…call me an interfering mother… call me a foolish old thing, if you will, but I *know*—I am *certain*—that Theodore would make a wonderful husband and a delightful father, if only he could keep away from the library for long enough to get to know a young woman of the right kind.'

'And how would you like me to help?'

'This is my scheme: I shall provide suitable young ladies and introduce them to him. What you will then do is ensure that they meet again, so that they further their acquaintance with one another. You will arrange for him to meet them several times more under the right sort of circumstances.'

'I'm still not certain that you need my services at all, Mrs Watt. Most mothers would invite their sons to tea parties or picnics or dinner parties or dances for this purpose.'

The older lady waved such ideas away.

'All of these I have tried. Either he refuses to come, or he comes and stands alone in a corner. He cannot speak to women. He cannot approach them. His academic work has erased all the pleasantries of normal conversation from his vocabulary.'

'But there are many such gentlemen in Cambridge, and most of them find a bride somehow.'

'This is true. Women find ways of compensating for even the greatest deficiencies of charm—I know that very well. I myself had to overcome some such limitations where Theodore's father was concerned. But young women seem to expect more these days. And dear Theodore is not getting any younger. He cannot dance—we tried lessons when he was younger, but he has very little co-ordination—he dislikes music and is really only interested in talking about fish. I have many times tried to explain to him that one might pretend an interest in something, for the purposes of conversation, for example, but poor Theodore cannot pretend anything. If he finds something dull, he says so. If he dislikes someone, he tells them that, too.'

'I can see that would be a disadvantage,' Lucia said. 'The last thing one expects at most gatherings is a straightforward declaration of honesty. And fish are rarely the centre of social conversation—except perhaps at dinner.'

'Quite!'

'I am still not entirely clear about the exact nature of the service you require.'

'Oh?' Mrs Watt looked alert.

'Am I to act as a match-maker?'

'Oh no! Perish the thought! *I* shall be the match-maker, if you must use such a common term; you shall be the… ' Mrs Watt looked at the ceiling, searching for the accurate term, the feathers on her hat slicing the office air behind her head. 'You shall be the *setter of the scene.*'

Chapter Two

'The setter of the scene?' Christabel raised a sceptical eyebrow as she poured her sister's cup of tea. 'What does that entail?'

They often took their tea in the tiny garden in Paradise Place, under the shade of a gnarled apple tree. 'A sum of money approximately three times higher than my normal fee, for one thing,' Lucia said.

'Excellent news. But who is willing to pay so much, and what are they expecting in return?'

'I am required to set the scene for romance to blossom between a young professor and ladies selected by his mother. His mother is paying. He can progress no further in his life without a bride, apparently. He is happy enough to meet and make conversation with eligible young ladies, but he then repeatedly fails to take any further action. My task is to ensure that he at least meets the ladies a second time and has the opportunity to further the acquaintance.'

'Is he a hopeless case?'

'He is only interested in fish.'

'Fish?'

'He is a professor of fish, or *ichthyology*, to use the correct term. I learnt it this morning.'

'Ah, so he is *solely* interested in fish. He is *floundering*, so you must find *salmon* to love him.'

Lucia sighed. 'Dreadful fish puns will not help the matter.'

'What of his appearance? Is that a factor?' Christabel asked, sipping her tea. 'I mean, he is a professor from a good family. Unless he is an absolute warthog, you'd think someone would have him.'

'Christabel! More respect for my paying clients, if you please.'

Christabel only shrugged.

'His mother admits that his hair is an unfortunate blond. Lovely on a three-year-old but not very manly in adulthood, in her view. And he is clean-shaven.'

'Oh dear. But otherwise, not especially hideous?'

'Who knows?'

'You need an objective opinion. Is he aware of this plan?'

'She didn't say, but I doubt it.'

'Someone reliable and inconspicuous is needed to assess his appearance.'

'That rules you out, Christabel.'

'I am reliable!'

'But you are not now, and never have been inconspicuous,' Lucia said, indicating her sister's outfit of red and white striped silk. Her sister only shrugged.

'You might send Ida Moss, perhaps. She was in the shop today. She is a good worker, but there is something almost invisible about Ida.'

'He follows a strict timetable: a walk at the same time

every afternoon, and so on. She will have no trouble finding him.'

Lucia sat back in her chair, enjoying the peace of the garden for a moment. A blackbird trilled his song from a nearby chimney, and bees buzzed in the honeysuckle over the wall.

'And how was the hat business today?'

It was her sister's turn to sigh and look grim. 'Birds! Three ladies came into the shop and declared they wanted birds—*whole* hummingbirds, to be precise—on their hats. They have all seen the same drawing in the *Ladies' Journal*.'

'Who would want a stuffed bird on their hat?'

'They are all the rage in Paris, according to *Mademoiselle Montmartre's* wretched millinery column. I have asked Ida to see what she can do with feathers and *papier mâché*. Meanwhile, my ladies will have to make do with her rather lovely varnished cherries instead. She is a peculiar little person, but very talented.'

'Perhaps you should call yourself *Mademoiselle Christabel* and write a millinery column in the Cambridge Journal. Then you could sing the praises of English fruit over foreign hummingbirds,' Lucia suggested.

Her sister glared, but another thought then cheered her. 'Mrs Doctor Lloyd settled her account today. I bought lamb chops.'

'Lamb chops!'

'And strawberries.'

'The extravagance!'

'For one evening only. Tomorrow we are back to tea and boiled eggs.'

Chapter Three

At the usual time of Professor Watt's afternoon stroll, the sun was glaring mercilessly onto the path over the bridge and out along the meadows known as the Backs.

Most visitors preferred shadier walks. The few ladies in evidence carried parasols to protect their complexions.

Miss Moss found the instructions repeating in her head. *Wait for the not-very-tall gentleman to leave by the side gate of Trinity College. He will probably be carrying a book. Do not hesitate or dawdle. Do not keep checking the time on your watch. Do not speak, just walk by and make a mental note of his appearance.*

The neck of her blouse grew damp. She adjusted a hatpin pressing against her scalp. Her white summer boots were laced too tightly at the ankle. *He will not come,* she told herself. *Why did I agree to do this?*

But even as the thought darkened her inner horizon, the small gate opened and a gentleman stepped through. He paused to latch the gate behind him, then turned to walk towards her.

Miss Moss felt a jerky palpitation in her chest. She

looked away and off to one side—the Trinity Hall side of the path, as it happened—glancing down at the stream that ran alongside the path, trying to remember the plan. Something caught her eye, and she stopped.

It was a large pale-bellied fish floating on the surface on its side. Its mouth, as she watched, extended repeatedly in a gaping O as it gasped for air. The fins against its sides paddled feebly. It was clearly trapped.

A movement made Ida look up, and she recognised the form of a heron on the opposite bank. It, too, had seen the ailing fish. The bird's cold eye and dagger-like beak focused with deadly intent on the fish's struggle.

'No!' Ida shouted, instinctively. 'Leave it! Go away!' She flapped her parasol over the railing and waved her arms. The bird looked angrily at her with yellow eyes before spreading wide wings and taking off, its spindly legs trailing. It flapped resentfully away over the college lawns.

The gentleman was close by. Ida was convinced now that the fish was breathing its last, and a moorhen was paddling towards it—another sharp-beaked bird.

'I'm afraid this fish is in danger!' she said.

He paused, then stepped alongside, glancing over the railing.

'A chub,' he said, 'and a fine specimen.'

'The heron was...'

'Yes. They go for the eyes.'

Ida shuddered. 'Is there nothing to be done for the poor creature?'

'It will certainly expire there. It has grounded itself on the mud and cannot breathe,' the gentleman said.

'Well, I cannot stand by and watch that happen.' Ida declared. 'I shall have to fetch someone. A gardener perhaps.'

'The gardeners will be at lunch,' he said. It was a flat statement of fact, so Ida was surprised when he followed it by removing his hat and shrugging off his jacket before bending to untie his shoes. Before she could say a word, he climbed the railing, dropped onto the narrow bank beside the path, then plunged into the stream. He immediately sank to the knees in a few inches of water and a foot or more of mud. Curling ribbons of grey-brown silt trailed downstream behind him. The moorhen, with a *kraak* of irritation, changed direction.

Rolling up his sleeves, he bent over the fish, and it was only now that Ida could appreciate the creature's true dimensions. It was a giant the size of a dinner plate. The gentleman splashed water over its body—to cool it, she supposed—then began to slide his hands under the fish before hesitating and looking up at Ida.

'I shall need assistance,' he told her. 'My aim is to lift the fish out, then carry it to the stream on the other side. Over there, the water is deeper.'

'Yes, I see,' Ida said.

'But I shall need both hands to climb out, so I shall have to hand it to someone there on the path.'

'Could I take it?'

'Is there no-one else?' he asked.

Ida must have looked disappointed because he added, 'I mean, is there no gentleman in sight? I ask only because it is a large fish and many ladies fear dirtying their clothes, and so on.'

'No gentleman is in sight. I am perfectly willing to help.'

'As you wish,' he said. He lifted the fish out of the mud, but then lost his grip and it slipped back in. For a moment, both of them looked on as the great chub paused in its breathing. 'It could be twenty years old,' he remarked.

The fish twitched and gasped silently again, much to their relief.

'If I spread your jacket here on the path, you could lift the poor thing onto that first,' Ida suggested.

She did so and the gentleman, moving this time very slowly, lifted the fish clear of the water, over the bank, beneath the lower railing and onto the silk lining of his jacket.

Ida, not knowing what else to do, held her parasol to shade it.

The gentleman now made several attempts to pull himself back onto the bank and out of the muddy stream, but each time he fell back and ended up deeper in the water. By the third attempt, he was well over his knees.

'Look,' he said. 'It may take me a while to extract myself. If that fish is to live, it must go into the other stream. Do you think you could call for help, or get it across yourself?'

Ida glanced in both directions up the path. It was still deserted. 'I shall take it myself,' she said.

Afraid of lifting the slippery fish and it falling from her grasp, she took the jacket by one sleeve and used it as a sled, hauling it across the path and over to the railing on the other side. Here she paused, unsure of her next move.

'You could just toss it,' the gentleman suggested. From his position in the opposite stream, his head was at the level of Ida's knees.

Tossing the fish did not seem a good idea to Ida. She did not feel like hurling the fish they had carefully rescued, only for the poor creature to ricochet off a railing or end up breathing its last in a clump of stinging nettles. There was nothing for it but to lower it carefully into the water, and there was no way of doing that without standing in the stream herself. She therefore clambered over the lower railing and dropped into the clear stream. There, with her white *broderie anglaise* dress floating around her knees, she reached across and pulled the fish on the jacket down the bank before easing it into the water.

The fish lay at the surface for several long moments, gasping, exactly as before.

'We were perhaps too late after all,' said the gentleman. He was now on the path, looking down. His lower legs and feet were covered in a rich slime that smelt pungently of decomposition. Clots and smears of the same substance splattered his shirt, his face and even the top of his head, which she could see clearly as he leaned over.

A gust of wind lifted the hat from Ida's head and flipped it before dropping it lightly onto the surface of the stream. It rotated and began to float away under the overhanging willows.

Both watched it for a moment, then, as they looked again at the fish, it flipped its tail, righted itself in the water, and slid away into the depths.

'There!' said Ida, smiling. The gentleman reached down and offered his hand. Accepting it, she stepped out of the water and climbed through the railing back onto the path.

'Well. Our good deed for the day is certainly done,' he said, 'but the damage to clothing has been considerable.'

Puddles were forming on the path where they stood.

'My college is just here,' he said. 'I'm sure the housekeeper could offer you assistance. I believe ladies fall into the river from punts occasionally. I imagine she has resources—spare clothing, and so on.'

It seemed improper to speculate further on matters concerning the clothing of ladies, so he stopped there. She had merry eyes, he noticed. Blue, perhaps.

'Thank you,' Ida said. 'I have a long walk. It would be good to dry my feet, at least.'

A passing young man stopped on his bicycle and handed Ida her hat, rescued from the stream, but also dripping, then cycled on.

'Mrs Budden, this lady has been in the water. She needs your assistance,' the gentleman announced when the housekeeper answered his knock.

Mrs B, large and unshakable, surveyed Ida, assessing the damage. 'I'll see what I can do, Professor,' she said. 'And if you leave your own wet things on your landing, I shall send someone up to collect them shortly. The mud may be a problem.'

'I shall leave you in Mrs Budden's hands, Miss... I apologise, we haven't been introduced.'

'Moss,' she said. Surprising him by holding out her hand in formal greeting. 'Ida Moss.'

'Ida Moss?' he repeated, 'I'm sure I know your name from somewhere.' He recovered himself, shook her hand and said, 'Theodore Watt.'

'*Professor* Watt?' she asked.

'Yes.' He seemed distracted.

'And your subject?'

'Natural Sciences. Ichthyology. That is to say, the study of...'

'Fish,' she said, 'thank you Professor, but I know what the word means.'

Chapter Four

'You are late, Theodore.'

Mrs Watt served tea at 4 o'clock sharp. It was half past now, and the tea had been in the pot too long. She poured it nonetheless and held out a cup of the dark and rather uninviting liquid. Her son had hurried in breathless and rumpled. His hair was damp and on end.

'Apologies, Mama. There was an incident.'

'Not a carriage accident, I hope?' Mrs Watt had a morbid fear of carriage accidents and scoured the newspapers daily for details of bolting horses and broken limbs to add to her evidence.

'No. It concerned a fish,'

'Oh, a fish!' His mother dismissed the thought with a wave of her hand. 'Now, Theodore, we have matters to discuss today. Important matters.'

By clever sleight of hand, Hanks, the maid, exchanged the old tea for a fresh cup without her mistress noticing and carried it over to Theodore, slipping a piece of shortbread into the saucer. She had known him since his infancy. They were conspirators of old.

'That will be all, thank you, Hanks.'

Hanks bobbed a stiff curtsey and left.

'You may not care for what I am about to tell you, my dear, but I'm sure you understand that I have your best interests at heart.'

He sipped tea and waited.

'I believe—well, you know this, we have discussed it on more than one occasion—I believe that you are at risk of letting the opportunity for marriage and a family pass you by.'

She watched him, but he did not react, so she continued. 'For several years, I have looked on as you began making excuses and turning invitations down. I have explained your absence many times at gatherings and parties—only last week... well, that is not important now. I have decided to take action. You need not concern yourself with the details. All I ask is that you join a small party for dinner here on a few evenings, and that you... ' She fidgeted and ran out of words.

'Yes?' he prompted.

'That you hold yourself open to furthering acquaintance with some ladies.' It was a carefully chosen form of words.

'Which ladies?'

'Appropriate ladies. Suitable ladies.'

'Oh good Lord, Mama!' He set his cup down and passed his hands over his face.

A silence fell in the room while Mrs Watt regrouped her thoughts and her son sighed and frowned at the pattern on the rug.

'Theodore, I am not to be moved this time. There is a

possibility—a possibility, I say, no more than that—of a very important position becoming vacant at your college. Don't ask me any more!'

Her son had no intention of doing so.

'That post, and many others like it, falls most comfortably upon a man of first class academic status who also has the wisdom of *broader* understanding. Someone whose outlook is coloured by the *breadth* of human experience.'

'I imagine it does,' Theo said.

'A man who knows about life, who can advise the younger members of the college—act as their counsellor in personal matters as well as academic ones. A *married* man, in other words,' his mother added, just to be sure.

'I see.'

'I am not alone in this belief. Only last week, Mrs Professor Gower-Price at Queens' mentioned that her husband's committee regularly favoured a married gentleman over a single one for certain positions.'

He nodded wearily.

'A senior tutorship—not that I have any special knowledge here—but a senior tutorship at a distinguished college is a step towards high office, as I'm sure you know. Look at Miles Kilmartin at Downing. I knew him as a young man. A good enough sort, but not especially talented. Once he had married Arabella and their family was growing, it gave him *gravitas*—and look where he ended up, Master of the College and a Member of the House of Lords!'

'And if I agree to your plan. If I come to dinner and—what was the other part?'

'To *hold yourself open* to further meetings.'

'Yes. If I agree to both those things, Mama, will you, in return, cease mentioning my bachelor status for at least five years?'

'Five years!'

'Three, then?'

'Two. I can say no more.'

'Two years. I accept. It is not that I am against the idea of marriage on principle. It is only that…'

His mother completed his sentence, '… the right young woman hasn't appeared. I know. And that is why I shall find and introduce her very soon.' To mask a look of triumph that might appear unseemly, she took a sip of tea, then shuddered. 'Ask Hanks to bring more tea, will you, dear? I don't know what she did to this.'

Watts carried the pot to the kitchen. As she put the kettle onto the range, Hanks said, 'I reckon the Mistress is after getting you wed, Master Theo.'

'She is, as usual,' he said. He was eating another piece of Hanks' excellent shortbread.

'She wants the best thing for you. And some grandchildren, of course.'

'I know.' He chewed for a moment, looking about him at the large familiar kitchen. The maid and her mistress occupied only corners of the big house now. Two old ladies together and apart.

'I should love some little'uns to come and visit as well. My word, I should like that. I could make them cakes and puddings that would light their little faces right up,' Hanks said.

Theo had fond memories of Hanks's cakes and puddings.

'Did you never think of marriage, Hanks? When you were younger?'

The kettle began to whistle. Hanks lifted it from the hotplate and poured water into the teapot.

How many thousands of times has she lifted that kettle? he wondered.

'I had one or two offers in my day,' she said, 'but I shilly-shallied. Then I got old and settled in my ways. I couldn't change now, not for anyone.'

She put the teapot on its tray. 'Find someone who takes your fancy while you're still young enough, Master Theo. Don't you shilly-shally or you'll end up like me. Alone on the shelf.'

'Do you regret it, Hanks?' he asked, taking the tray to the door.

'Bless you, no. I'm past caring. I've got my niece and her little lad. That'll do me.'

Chapter Five

The impracticality of learned men never ceased to amaze and entertain college staff, especially the porters. Most of them had jolly pub stories of professors who didn't seem to understand how keys or taps worked, or who went out in all weathers in slippers or gave lectures in their nightcaps. When Professor Watt asked Bill Parker how one might find an address for someone who lived in the city, it was most satisfying for Bill to reach under the counter in the Porters' Lodge, find the Cambridge City Directory and place it in front of him.

'In there. You just look at the names at the back. Alphabetical. All the shops and everything's there too.'

The professor was impressed. 'How very convenient. Thank you Bill. May I borrow this?'

'Keep it for as long as you need it, Professor. I have another copy.'

'That's one who doesn't know if it's Christmas or Easter,' he told his junior as they watched the professor wander away, still reading the directory. To add to their amusement, he was clutching a ladies' parasol. It had been left with his expertly restored clothing outside his rooms that morning.

The address he found was not one the Professor knew, but a street map was part of the marvellous directory, so after pausing in the middle of Old Court to consult it, he changed direction and set off for the centre of the city.

Under their colourful canvas shades, the market traders were busy, but the heat still kept most people from the streets. Towards the railway, rows of smaller shops and businesses seemed busier. People sat outside their front doors fanning themselves and passing the time of day on the shady side of the street. Dogs scratched and rolled; children played hopscotch and chasing games. Each street led into the next and the houses grew smaller at each junction until he stood at the end of a long terraced row where each house seemed barely wider than the span of his arms. Some had a tiny patch of front garden, but most had front doors opening straight off the street.

There were few Mosses listed in the directory. Here, at 15 Cooper Street, there seemed to be two: Mr F. and Miss I. The professor knocked.

A shout came from inside. An old man's voice, 'Who is it? What is it you want?'

The professor was not used to being shouted at through closed doors. He stepped back and waited.

'Who are you?' the voice bellowed from directly behind the door. 'Go away!'

'Mr Moss?'

'Get away with you!'

'Mr Moss? I was wondering whether a Miss Ida Moss lives here.'

'What?' cried the voice. 'Who are you?'

'I am Professor Watt,' he said, speaking loudly and directing his remarks to the door at ear height.

'What?' the voice bellowed from inside.

'Watt! I am Professor Watt, of Trinity College.' It was foolish declaring his credentials to the door knocker, but there seemed no alternative.

'Oh, *Professor*, is it now?' cried the voice from inside. 'Off with you all the same!'

Provoked, Watt stepped back. At this moment, a boy appeared behind him on the pavement. He carried three or four books tied together with a strap. He wore a large sun hat and despite the heat, a scarf covered his face so that only his eyes could be seen.

'My Grandfather will not open the door to strangers,' he said, his voice muffled by the scarf. 'We never do. I could take a message if you have one.' His tone was informative rather than hostile.

The professor looked down at the child in confusion.

'I am hoping to return this umbrella.' He showed him.

'That is a parasol,' the child told him, 'not an umbrella.'

'Forgive me. I am hoping to return this *parasol* to Miss Ida Watt. I believe it belongs to her. Does she live here?'

'We don't tell things to strangers,' the boy said.

The door flew open, revealing an elderly man in his shirtsleeves. He wore a waistcoat and had a tea towel over one shoulder. 'Come in, boy, come in. Your tea's ready for you,' he said to the child, ushering him in.

The boy stepped past the old man and disappeared into the shadowy interior. The professor looked after the child and was surprised at how far back the house extended and how welcoming the little home appeared. 'He has a parasol,' the boy added over his shoulder.

'I can see that for myself,' the old man said.

'I was hoping to return it to Miss Ida Watt, but perhaps I have the wrong address.'

The old man examined the parasol and its bearer with frowning suspicion.

'Leave it here, if you care to,' he finally said.

'So Miss Ida Watt does live here?'

'Leave it here, I say, if you wish.'

With a final glare, the old man closed his front door.

Professor Watt stood looking at the door's brass handle for several minutes, trying to work out what to do next. To leave the parasol outside the front door was to leave it on the pavement, where any passer-by could carry it away. This he did not intend to risk. On the other hand, to take it away was to fail to restore it to Miss Moss, and thus to fail in the small quest he had set himself.

He was still pondering all this when the door opened again, but only by a crack, and a child's open hand was extended. It hovered like a pale starfish against the dark front door, then wriggled, expressing impatience. The professor put the parasol's handle into the hand, which grasped it and quickly pulled it inside, closing the door.

The professor strode back to his college through first the little streets, then the broader ones feeling more triumphant than really made sense. The smell of roses and newly mown grass was everywhere.

Chapter Six

If he examined it at all, the professor attributed his sudden vigorous enjoyment of a summer evening's walk through town to successfully returning Miss Moss's lost property. He returned the little directory to the porter's lodge and reached his rooms just as the bell sounded for dinner.

At this time of year, after degrees had been presented and all the new graduates were gone, the high table was quiet. Only the permanent residents and one or two visitors or guests were to be expected, so Watt was pleased when his table companions turned out to be Herr Doktor Markus Brünerhof, a German scholar, and a historian, Dr William Halfpenny. A pleasant dinner's conversation lay ahead.

'We don't often see you at high table in the summer, Dr Brünerhof,' Watt remarked, as soon as Grace had been said.

Brünerhof, the senior man by at least twenty years, smiled as he flapped a table napkin onto his knees. 'My family keeps me at home, as a rule, but they are at Yarmouth for a short vacation.'

'You were not tempted to join them? The sea air is excellent there, I believe.'

'I am finishing something for publication. Now that they are gone, however, I find the house is so very quiet that I can hardly concentrate. When one has a large family, one becomes accustomed to a great deal of activity. Children running about, and so on. Everything now seems far too silent.'

The soup was brought. Wine was poured. They began to eat.

'So, you will take a vacation yourself, Professor Watt?' the German asked.

'I am also preparing something for publication. I have no plans for the summer other than that,' Watt told him.

They ate companionably for a few moments, the bright evening light from the high windows filtering through the dining hall's elaborate roof beams around them. It was only then that the professor observed the lack of movement from Halfpenny on his right. Dr Halfpenny sat looking into his soup but made no move to eat it.

'The soup is not to your taste, Halfpenny?'

Halfpenny shuddered and seemed to wake from distraction. 'I am not myself,' he muttered.

'You are not well?'

'I have had bad news.'

'I'm sorry to hear that,' Watt said.

Halfpenny lifted his head and stared unseeing across the grandeur of the almost empty dining hall.

'I don't know what to do,' he declared.

Watt could only look at him in concern. His colleague was pale beneath his beard. His eyes red-rimmed. 'I have heard today that Gwendolyn—you know her, I have mentioned her before—Gwendolyn is to move to Heidelberg.

Her father has a post there. A prestigious new appointment. Naturally, he will take the family. They will be gone by August. *Heidelberg!*' he said, in tones of despair. 'I shall lose her.'

Watt, though unsettled by his companion's evident woe, was at a loss as to what to say. Not so Dr Brünerhof.

'You speak of Dr Hurst's daughter?' he enquired. 'His eldest? I know the Hursts well.'

'You do?' The information brought light into Halfpenny's eye. He looked past Watt at the German.

'Of course. A very good family. You are engaged to be married to Gwendolyn?'

'No. Not engaged. I did approach her father, but he— well, I had so little to offer. My family is not wealthy. I have only a little teaching. It is insufficient.'

'He rejects you?' asked the German, speaking loudly, but concentrating on his soup.

'Utterly.'

The professor felt uncomfortably out of his depth. It was most unusual for such personal matters to come under discussion at high table. In term time it would be unthinkable, but matters changed, somehow, in the summer.

'And she?' Brünerhof continued. 'What does the young woman herself think of you?'

'She and I... We... We have a good understanding,' Halfpenny answered, with difficulty.

Brünerhof was eating with determination. The questions so far had been directed to Halfpenny without looking up.

Watt spooned consommé from his dish. They were speaking across him.

'An *understanding*?' cried the German. 'This is too British! Excuse me, gentlemen, but the rigid formality of your countrymen is extraordinary to me. *Do you love this young woman, or not, Halfpenny?*'

A college servant, pouring wine at that moment, leaned in to hear the reply.

'I love her entirely, as it happens. She is the light of my life. There. I have said it.'

Brünerhof took a draft of wine and raised his glass to Halfpenny. 'Congratulations. Young men should be more brave! Faint hearts do not win young ladies—or whatever the saying is. Do not accept her father's decision! You must fight for her!'

'That's all very well...'

But Dr Brünerhof, now on his second glass, was hitting his stride. 'I myself had a great struggle to secure the hand of my wife—my Anna-Maria. Her father did not want his daughter to marry a scholar with nothing but a trunk of books and the boots he stood up in. He set the dogs on me! Many times I had their teeth-biting marks on my behind!' He chuckled at the memory.

'How did you persuade him? How did you win the day?' Halfpenny asked.

Watt, redundant in this conversation, could only eat and listen.

'Ach, I do not know. I cannot tell you. Only this. I *knew* that dear girl must be mine. I saw our life together with complete certainty. *Certainty*. I never doubted. I was in my twenties only, but I saw it clearly. Marriage, children, a whole life with Anna-Maria at my side. No other life was possible to me. And so it has been. A good life and eight fine children. So you see, I could not be stopped. Eventually, her father saw this. He was not happy, but he could not doubt my great determination and sincerity. And her mother helped. She liked me. That is a great advantage.' Brünerhof wiped his beard with his napkin. 'You should try speaking to Mrs Hurst. She is a woman of good sense.'

Untouched soup was taken from Halfpenny's place and replaced with slices of beef to which new potatoes and peas were swiftly added. He picked up his knife and fork. 'I am afraid that if she travels to Heidelberg, she will marry a German,' he said. 'My fears are well justified if they are all as determined as you were, Doctor, when it comes to marriage.' He smiled for the first time.

'We German men have advantages when it comes to matters of the heart,' Brünerhof said, spearing a buttery new potato. 'We do not hide from emotions like Englishmen. The feelings of our hearts are familiar to us, not hidden away in some dusty English cupboard. Your own dear Queen was well aware of this when she married Prince Albert, of course.'

'Are we really so lacking in sentiment?' Watt put in.

'It is not that we lack sentiment exactly,' Halfpenny said. 'Only that we handle sentimental feelings clumsily, and therefore lack the courage to act on them. I think Dr Brünerhof has rather a good point.' He turned to his dinner and began to eat.

It was still warm when the dinner ended. Watt and Halfpenny, having wished their German companion good night, took a stroll through the Fellow's Garden where a gentle breeze cast the scent of acacia and honeysuckle about them. One or two glasses of the '88 port had been taken, and Halfpenny was so buoyed up by this, and by Brünerhof's encouragement at dinner, that he could hardly stop waving his arms and exclaiming at the beauty of the trees and the wonder of the evening.

'I shall do it, Watt,' he said. 'I shall take a stand! Gwendolyn shall be mine!'

'Good luck to you, Halfpenny.'

'And what of you? Is there no lady on your horizons?'

'There will be, if my mother has anything to do with it.'

'Your mother is seeking a match for you, then?'

'She is trying to. She believes I cannot live a full life or advance any further in the College unless I am a married man.'

'Senior college men used never to marry at all.'

'Such facts mean little to her.'

'She sees you as a future Senior Tutor, perhaps?'

'I've no idea.'

'She does! Your mother is always alert to the college grapevine. Is the Senior Tutorship coming up? It would be a step up, you can't deny it. A fine college house, staff, you'd be set for life. Earnest, respectable, sober. You'd make a fine Senior Tutor.'

'This is nothing but foolish speculation.'

'I did hear that Rathbone got himself into bad odour with one or two people. The Dean of Chapel does not care for him. There was a whiff of scandal about that foreign lady. Do you remember? The divorcée! Perhaps your mother knows something. Perhaps he is going to step aside.'

Watt sighed. He disliked college gossip.

'You did walk out with a young lady once. Miss Tipton, wasn't it?'

'You and I were undergraduates, Halfpenny. It was an age ago.'

'She broke your heart?'

'She married.'

'She did break your heart!'

'I think I felt mostly relief.'

'It was not true love, then,' Will said, throwing himself down on a bench and looking up at the stars. 'There has been no other?'

'I find women—most women—inscrutable, and, to be perfectly honest, I find quite a lot of them over-talkative and irritating. I prefer my work.'

'It's easier if you have sisters. They treated me appallingly, but at least I grew up understanding a little of the female mind.'

'I shall stick to fossils,' Watt said, looking up at the sky himself.

'Fossils never talk too much, I suppose,' Halfpenny said. 'Or challenge your comfortable daily existence.'

'Comfortable? Nonsense! New fossils are found every day. I have many challenges.'

'But nothing that would change your perspective on life?'

'Why should I want to do that?'

'You don't fear becoming set in your ways? You don't wonder whether the pattern of your life in thirty years' time might not end up exactly the same in every detail as your life now?'

'I should be perfectly happy if it did.'

'What a stick in the mud you are, Theo.'

The idea of being stuck in the mud suddenly brought the rescue of the chub and Miss Moss into his mind.

'Am I?'

'When did you last try something new?'

'What kind of thing?'

'Anything. Anything whatever?'

Watt thought again of Miss Moss. Her blue eyes smiling at him as the rivery tidemark dried into her dress and mud caked his trousers. That had been something new.

'You see!' Halfpenny went on, 'You have made no change in your life for so long that you can hardly imagine one.'

'What sort of change is needed?'

'A novel pursuit, for example. Something energetic. Cricket or swimming in the river. You might even try riding a bicycle.'

'I avoid cricket for good reason. I am no good at catching a ball.'

'And swimming?'

Watt said nothing. He looked across the dark garden. Moths were out and distantly a nightingale was beginning a bubbling stream of song. 'No. I cannot swim. I was not a healthy child. They kept me out of the water.'

'I could teach you. We could start in the pool at Emmanuel.'

'What? No!'

'I challenge you, Watt. This summer, try something new. Prove to yourself that you are not so rigidly unchangeable as your mother suspects.'

Halfpenny was grinning up at the stars.

'And what is your own challenge?' Watt asked.

'To win fair Gwendolyn's hand, of course.'

Trying to sleep—the night was steamy and his windows only drew in even hotter air—Watt turned the evening's conversation over in his mind. When he fell asleep at last, he dreamt he was swallowed whole by a giant chub.

Chapter Seven

Mrs Watt sank into Lucia Venables' office chair, gasping and fanning herself with her gloves. 'Whose is that cat on the stairs? The creature swiped its claws at my hat as I passed. I might have fallen to my death! It is a threat to life and limb.'

'I shall speak to my landlady,' Lucia said. Over her client's shoulder, she could see a nonchalant Blossom licking a front paw on the landing.

'To business,' Mrs Watt declared. 'My first dinner party is this evening. I have invited Miss McCreedy-Roberts to meet my son. They will be introduced and sit next to one another at dinner. I shall encourage them into the garden *alone* in the course of the evening, and I shall ensure that my son's praises are sung loud and long before her mother and all the other guests.'

'McCreedy-Roberts, you say?' Lucia wrote the name into her notebook.

'Yes. Tatiana McCreedy-Roberts. I know her parents

well. Her mother has Russian connections—hence the rather unfortunate foreign name, but she is a well brought-up young woman. Perhaps a little young, but charming and mercifully, not in the least scholarly. I dread scholarly women—they ruin their looks with all that squinting over books. Where would they be if bride and groom both spent all their time in libraries? I am firmly of the belief that a scholarly man needs a good practical wife.'

'And I am to ensure that Professor Watt and Miss McCreedy-Roberts meet again 'by accident' as soon as possible?'

'Exactly. They will have made a good start over dinner. You should bring them together in such a way as to encourage a deepening of the acquaintance. My son is very unlikely to take the initiative. He never does. He spends a perfectly enjoyable evening in conversation with a charming young woman, but then it never occurs to him to make any further arrangements. And since he refuses most of my invitations, unless we take steps, he never will. How shall we do it?'

'Does this lady like hats?'

'I imagine so. Most young ladies like hats.'

'Then I shall give you this card,' she produced one of her sister's, 'and you will pass it to her over dinner by way of recommending the shop. She will then visit the shop, and I shall take it from there. I know the professor's movements. I'm sure I can arrange a meeting.'

Mrs Watt considered this. 'They need a decent interval together.'

'I was thinking of a carriage drive or a long country walk.'

'That sounds excellent. I leave the details in your hands,

Miss Venables. And now I must go and oversee preparations for dinner. Is that animal out of the way?'

Lucia hurried to the landing. Blossom had vanished.

'I will happily sell her a hat, if you bring her to the shop,' Christabel said over tea in their apartment on the top floor later, 'but how do you plan to arrange a meeting between the professor and this double-barrelled lady?'

'I shall strike up a conversation with her. She does not know Cambridge, so I shall recommend something that will coincide with the professor on one of his regular jaunts. Her mother will then bow out, leaving them together.'

'What a fuss this all is,' Christabel said. 'Why not tell the man frankly that he needs to take the initiative and allow him to take charge of his own sentimental enterprises?'

'Because then I will not earn my fee, for one thing.'

'Well, that is a point. But really, talk about leading a horse to water.'

'This horse will drink. He will! He only needs a little encouragement. Or so his mother contends.'

'He may not be the marrying kind.'

'We are not forcing him into marriage against his will. His mother is simply smoothing his way. And I am helping. She has paid me a third of the fee already. I bought us a bloater for supper.'

'A bloater *each*?'

'No, greedy! One to share, but I can also offer a gooseberry tart from Franklin's.'

'Plenty more fish in the sea, I suppose, if the professor doesn't care for this double-barrelled one.'

At this point her sister thew a cushion.

Ida came through from the back workroom when she heard the bell. She was alone in the shop that afternoon.

'Ah,' said the customer, looking anxious, 'I usually speak to Miss Venables.'

Ida already knew well enough that the buying of hats was something certain ladies found intimidating. Others of every age and appearance revelled in it, cheerful in front of the mirrors, turning this way and that to admire themselves, but shy ladies found it a worse trial than the dentist and needed reassurance. It was never easy to predict which of these camps ladies would fall into.

'Perhaps I could help?' Ida suggested.

'I should prefer it if you would continue with your work and allow me to examine your summer straws alone, if that is possible,' said the customer. She removed the hat she was wearing—an expensive one, Ida noted—and began to look around. She was middle-aged, with her grey hair coming loose from its fastenings. Her maid was clearly not very skilful with the hair pins at the back. Or perhaps the lady was concerned with matters other than her hair.

Ida waited at the back of the showroom where a pile of tissue paper had been left on the counter. Miss Venables complained regularly about this paper. It was costly and delicately patterned, but something had spilled on it, so the leaves were sticking together. For want of other occupation—her half-made bird had been left in the back room—Ida began trying to peel the fine layers apart. The customer moved shyly about, examining hats, trying one or two on.

Separating the papers was a satisfying activity. Ida eased several sheets apart, then fetched the steam kettle and tried steaming others. She had rescued more than a dozen and was absorbed in the activity when she realised the customer was watching her.

'You do that very skilfully,' she remarked.

'I'm so sorry, Madam,' Ida said, hastening to wipe her hands on her apron. 'I was distracted. Can I bring you anything?'

'You are generally good with your hands? You have a facility for delicate work?' asked the lady.

'Well, yes, but...'

'I am looking for someone. Someone with a very gentle touch. To work in the library.'

Ida looked at her in confusion.

'We have a collection of manuscripts. They are so delicate. So ancient. Many of them are priceless, irreplaceable, but many have been poorly stored. Dampened and compressed. They adhere. Exactly like that tissue paper.'

Ida looked down at the tissue paper and back at the lady.

'I'm not explaining this well,' the customer said. 'I am Caroline McAdam. I work with Dr Solomon at the University Library. We need a helper. Someone who can help us separate and conserve parchment fragments. There would be a payment, obviously.'

'What happens to the pieces once they are separated?' Ida asked.

'We—a small team of us—we try to decipher the text and, if possible, make a translation. Do you have any education? I presume you can read and write.'

'I can, yes.'

'You know some French, perhaps? I imagine it would be useful in the millinery business.'

'A little French. A little German. Greek. Latin. My Arabic is not so strong.'

The lady rocked on her feet. 'You are a linguist?'

'I had a scholarship. It was a long time ago.'

'Good heavens!' The lady said. 'My dear, you are exactly what we need.'

'I have a family. My time is not my own.'

'Oh. You are married?'

'I live with my father and my nephew.'

'You are their sole support?'

'Yes. They rely on me.'

'I see. But you could spare some time? We would train you. You could work the hours you chose. There are so many fragments. Thousands of them. We need help, but so few people can do this work. The remuneration would not be great, but it would be steady. There are enough broken pieces to keep us busy for several centuries. Please say you will consider it at least.'

The door bell rang suddenly as Christabel returned. 'Ah, Mrs McAdam, my apologies if I kept you waiting.'

'Not at all,' Mrs McAdam said. 'But I must warn you that I intend to steal away this member of your staff.'

Dr Solomon's great room in the University Library was the strangest place Ida had ever seen. It was the size of a chapel with a high ceiling beamed in dark oak. Arched windows threw angled shafts of light over boxes, benches and tables ranged over three quarters of the floor space. Strewn, piled and spread on these surfaces, were what looked at first like rags. But these were the precious manuscripts. When the porter left her at the door, she stood bewildered. What a task! Was it even humanly possible to sort, save, and decipher so many thousands of pieces? Where could anyone even begin?

Only after standing there for some minutes did she realise that a tall figure was sitting at a table at the far end, bent over something.

'Doctor Solomon?' she asked.

He looked up. He wore two pairs of glasses. One on his head, one over his eyes. He had a lion's mane of curled grey hair and a beard to match. He strode over and shook her warmly by the hand, towering above her.

'You are Miss Moss, yes? From the hat shop!' It seemed to delight him.

'Yes. You must be Doctor Solomon.'

'Yes, yes. And here you see the precious treasures.' He spread his arms, beaming with pride. 'You see? We take a piece. We try to read it. If we can read it, we translate. We take another piece, we try to read that. We try to translate. Perhaps we find it is connected to one we already know. Once in a while a few words come together. Once in a while—oh but very rarely, very rarely—we complete a whole sentence. We have everything here: notes to the butcher; prayers; love letters; prescriptions for medicines; pieces of the scriptures, curses, charms, begging letters, poems. We never know what we will find. Some are eight hundred years old,' he said. 'Truly, Miss Moss, I am the luckiest man in the world.'

Ida was touched by this great scholar's simple joy in his Herculean task. The scruffy rags heaped in dusty boxes were transformed, as he spoke, into treasures in her eyes too.

'So,' he continued, 'By some miracle Mrs McAdam has succeeded in persuading the church groups and religious foundations who support our work to fund a junior assistant's position. We must strike while the iron is hot. When can you start? Whatever you can do, we will be grateful. I shall teach you. Mrs McAdam will teach you also. Can you come tomorrow?'

'I thought you might want to see my examination certificates, and so forth,' Ida said.

'Caroline has told us all we need to know. Do you think you would like to join us here?'

'I should like it very much indeed.'

Dr Solomon was pleased.

'Excellent! It is engrossing work. I know you will enjoy it, but I always give a warning: it is tempting to bury oneself here—in these fragments of the lives of others. I have made this mistake myself in the past and neglected my dear ones. We should not do so. We must remember to live our own lives as well, Miss Moss, yes?'

'It is easier to piece together the lives of others, perhaps,' Ida said.

'Sometimes it is. But you are young, remember? These records teach us that human life is short. You agree, yes? Each moment of our life is a precious gift.'

She wanted to agree with Dr Solomon, who, standing in a dusty beam of sunlight, looked like a bespectacled Old Testament prophet. She could, however, think of plenty of moments in her past that had not been precious, and had not been gifts. Dr Solomon saw the change in her expression and noted it.

He spent an hour showing her the sorting system and the methods of identifying and recording the fragments. He showed her the steam kettle they used to separate compressed and damaged pieces. He showed her the drying table and the box of instruments and brushes. He showed her where the linen aprons were hung.

Just picturing the room in the library, just reminding herself of its calm, purposeful activity and knowing she could be part of it, made Ida smile to herself all the way home to Cooper Street.

Chapter Eight

Watt woke at dawn, his mind hopping and cartwheeling with ideas. There was no chance of further rest. He was frequently at his desk hours before the rest of the college opened a sleepy eye. The proofs of his manuscript lay waiting, but proofreading was out of the question. A perfect summer's day was already smiling on Cambridge. He must walk.

Raising the blinds as he left, he pulled too sharply and the small wooden acorn that hung on the drawstring as a weight split into two pieces in his hand. He put the pieces in his pocket for the housekeeper and trotted down the worn stone steps of the ancient building, across the courtyard and out into the street.

His favourite brisk walk took him over Garret Hostel bridge and along the Backs to the Mill Pond and the meadows beyond. He paused at the point where the chub had been rescued and looked into the stream on either side, but saw only a mallard dabbling along the grassy bank. Silvery light sparkled on the surface of the water.

It would not be true to say that all streets in Cambridge lead to the market, but most do, so after a brisk circular walk, he found himself there. Few customers were about at this hour, but it was lively, with traders calling to one another as they raised awnings and set out their displays. Carts from farms outside the city were delivering; baskets, crates, bundles and boxes of all descriptions being hefted on strong shoulders across the cobbled square in front of Great St Mary's church. A few stalls were trading already, among them a fish stall where he paused to examine a fine row of crabs with their pincers tied, and a dozen eels writhing in a bucket.

The stall next to the fishmonger sold small decorative items. There were a few willow pattern plates, most of which had a chip, and some tiny glasses which might prettily serve a guest a thimbleful of sherry. As he glanced over, he noticed, lying between a small toby jug and a tortoiseshell hairbrush losing its bristles, an acorn exactly similar to the broken one he had in his pocket. He reached for it, but so at the same moment, did another hand. His was the hand that grasped the little acorn first, causing the other hand—a lady's—to withdraw instantly, as if it had been bitten.

'I beg your pardon,' he turned to say. 'Oh, it is Miss Moss!'

A shadow of fear passed over her face before she recognised him and smiled in relief.

'Professor Watt,' she said.

'I apologise if I appeared to snatch this away.' He opened his hand, and both looked closely at the acorn in his palm.

'Perhaps you need it urgently?' she suggested.

'Not at all. I was only curious. But you, perhaps you are greatly in need of a wooden acorn yourself.'

'I thought it looked like a hummingbird's head,' she said.

He looked at the acorn again. 'It would be rather larger than most hummingbirds' heads, I think,' he said. 'Their heads would be more the size of this bead, for example.' He showed her a much smaller glass bead.

'The bead is too heavy. The acorn is lighter and I could cut it down. It might even make two.'

'You plan to make two hummingbirds?'

'More,' she said, 'half a dozen at least.'

'With feathers and so on?' he inquired.

'Yes. I shall paint pigeon feathers and use small beads for the eyes.'

'Real hummingbird feathers are rare and very beautiful. They were used as currency at one time, on certain Polynesian islands.'

'I know,' she said. 'But now, rather sadly, they are used on ladies' hats.'

'You make hats?'

'Decorations for hats. Hummingbirds are all the rage.'

'Well,' he said. 'I did not know that.'

They were interrupted by the impatient voice of the stall holder. 'Will you be buying that?' she demanded.

'Yes,' they said together.

The professor, as it turned out, had no money about him. It was Miss Moss who had her purse to hand and paid the penny. He placed the acorn in her hand with a bow.

'But this leaves you an acorn short,' she said. She looked up at him, and her face was bright with a smile.

'I am almost certain the budget of Trinity College will run to a replacement,' he told her. 'Mrs Budden probably has a box of them.'

They took a few steps. The crabs and eels were still on

the fishmonger's stall. They had now been joined by a large cod, baskets of mussels, and rows of kippers.

'Eels are the most fascinating creatures, Miss Moss. Perhaps you know about them already?'

'I have certainly eaten them.'

'A delicacy.'

'Yes. Very popular in London.'

'You are a Londoner yourself?'

'Originally, yes. But apart from being served in jelly, what is so interesting about eels?'

'I hardly know where to start,' he said. 'They are among the most mysterious creatures on earth.'

'Really? Why?'

'People have tried for centuries to work out how it is that they breed. It is a question that has defeated science so far. There are many theories. The Egyptians believed they were created by the heat of the sun on the mud of the Nile. I've spoken to country people who still think they come from hairs that fall into the river from horses' tails.'

She looked surprised at this. 'And what do you think?' she asked him.

'Me? Oh, I am no expert on eels, but their mysteriousness is appealing. I dissected them as an undergraduate. They have no reproductive organs.' Hearing his own remark, he suddenly wondered if such information might be unacceptable to a lady and looked at her anxiously for signs of outrage or disgust. He was relieved to see that no such signs were evident.

'Was it you who returned the parasol, Professor?' she asked, still looking into the bucket of eels.

'It was,' he said it with a certain pride, but then he noticed that she was frowning.

'I thought you might have sent a college servant,' she

said. 'It was kind of you to bring it yourself. My father may have appeared ungracious or even rude. I'm sorry if that was so. My family does not welcome callers, as a general rule.'

'I trust I did not disturb anyone,' he said.

She turned away from him. 'We have our reasons, Professor Watt. It would be better if you did not return.'

'As you wish,' he said. It surprised him that he felt this as a blow to the chest.

She no longer looked at him, addressing her words to the pavement. 'I am expected elsewhere.' She gestured away from the market towards Rose Crescent, nodded to him briefly, and turned away.

A cloud came over the sun as Watt watched the growing crowd close around her. He was seized by the thought that he must not, on any account, allow the meeting to end on that note, but also that he had no reason to pursue her, and no right to detain her longer. Irritated by his own indecision, he thrust his hands into his pockets and, as he did so, found the broken acorn. Newly determined, he hurried after her.

'Miss Moss, wait!' he said. 'Perhaps these would be of use?' He showed her the two halves of the broken acorn from his pocket. 'You could make two more out of this and so double your output of hummingbirds.'

Her shoulders had tensed at the sound of her name, but she relaxed now and looked at the small broken offering of the split acorn he held out on his palm.

'I could.'

'Take them as a gift, I beg you.'

'No, not as a gift. I cannot accept a gift, Professor.'

'Oh come now. It is nothing of value. Surely you are not too proud to accept this broken thing.'

'Far too proud. I must pay you a fair price.'

He could see there was no persuading her.

'Then I shall charge you a farthing. That seems fair.'

'No, wait,' she said. 'You wanted the whole one. I need one in two pieces. We could simply exchange my whole acorn for your broken one.' She began to search her purse for it. She had very likeable hands, he thought. Neat and nimble.

'No, Miss Moss. A broken acorn is not a fair exchange for a whole one, and I did not contribute to the cost of the whole one either.'

'Then I shall charge *you* a farthing,' she said.

'Agreed. I have no money about me, however, if you recall.'

'Consider it a loan.'

'I could bring payment to the hat shop. Which is it?'

She looked wary and said with some reluctance, 'Madame Ladoré in Paradise Place.'

'You are there every day?'

'No. But you could leave it with Miss Venables, the owner.'

'Miss Venables? The owner is not called Madame Ladoré?'

'It is a professional title only. French names are popular for hat shops.'

'French names and hummingbirds. I am learning a lot about millinery today.'

'And making light of it, too, I rather think.'

'I would not dream of making light of the manner in which someone earns a living. No indeed,' he said.

She looked over at his face, unable to judge how serious he was.

'Studying fish could be seen as risible in some quarters,' she told him.

'A profoundly shocking thought,' he said, smiling, 'but no doubt you are right.'

'Besides,' she added, 'millinery is not the only way I earn a living.'

'You have other strings to your bow besides Madame Ladoré and the hat trade?'

'I am employed in the University Library.'

This answer took him by surprise, which gave her some satisfaction.

'How are your skills employed there?'

'I am assisting Doctor Solomon with his ancient manuscripts. Do you know him?'

'Everyone knows Doctor Solomon and his work.' He was looking at her in astonishment, but she continued walking. Enthusiasm for her new employment brought sudden energy to her stride. He had to bound to keep up.

'I am new to it, but it is wonderful work,' she told him. 'So far, I have only used the steamer to part tiny fragments that have been dampened over the years and compressed together. They are hundreds and hundreds of years old. Some had marks on them, but many were darkened and illegible. If I acquire the skills, I might be able to read a few lines of writing and perhaps even make a translation one day. Some fragments are from the earliest scriptures. It is an extraordinary privilege even to see them! They are treasures. There is so much to learn. I have Latin and Greek, but only a little Arabic. Mrs McAdam has already offered to teach me Syriac and Aramaic.' She paused, a little breathless.

They had reached Green Street already.

'You did not learn Greek and Latin in a hat shop, surely, Miss Moss?' he asked, drawing alongside.

'Of course I did! Hat shops are little universities for ladies,' she said. 'Did you not know? Hardly a day goes by without a class in Hebrew or ancient Persian.'

'I was not aware,' he said, but then saw her expression. 'Oh, you are not serious.'

'No, I am not serious, Professor Watt. As far as I know, very few language lessons take place in milliners' shops.'

When she turned, she was laughing. He was near enough to see her eyes shine and the precise way a smile turned up the very corner of her mouth—an image that revisited his mind at intervals for several days.

Chapter Nine

'You must have some notion of the kind of lady you find appealing.' Halfpenny said.

'Appealing?'

'Oh, come now, Watt. We are not talking about furniture or carpets. You must have some preferences where the female of the species is concerned.'

They were making their way across the grass to the swimming pool set in the lawns at Emmanuel College.

Watt only looked perplexed.

'Do you like someone tall, or a shorter lady, for example?' Halfpenny continued, beginning on what he thought might be neutral enough territory.

'I have never given her height a thought,' Watt told him.

'I myself prefer a smaller lady. Gwendolyn is petite.'

'I have no opinion to offer on the matter of a lady's stature.'

'You make this difficult, old man.'

'Not intentionally. I clearly do not think about these things in the same way as you do.'

Halfpenny walked ahead, 'What of the colour of her hair? You can be honest with me. It goes no further.'

'I really am not very interested in someone's hair.'

Halfpenny led them to a changing hut and began throwing off his clothes. 'I am for dark hair myself, every time. Gwendolyn's is a quite marvellous chestnut.'

Watt frowned. 'I think I care more about character.' He unrolled his towel to reveal a newly bought swimming costume and took off his jacket.

'Well, what would you look for there? In the character of your ideal lady?'

'I should like her to be…'

Halfpenny had cast his clothes off without hesitation and now pulled his own costume on. It was faded with the use of many summers. Watt, unfamiliar with the rituals of swimming, undressed more deliberately. His own swimming costume had a conspicuously newly minted quality, he suddenly felt.

'Yes?' Halfpenny urged.

'Amusing. I should like her to be amusing. Interesting. Intriguing, even. I should prefer it if she were not an open book. I would rather not be able to tell everything about her immediately.'

'You want a sort of research project?' Halfpenny looked doubtful.

'I suppose I do,' Watt said, 'I imagine it would be satisfying to spend one's life discovering the person one marries.'

'What a peculiar idea!' Halfpenny said, leading the way out of the changing hut. 'I hope to know everything—well, almost everything—about Gwendolyn by the time we marry.'

Ten minutes later, three bathers were kneeling in a circle around Watt's prone figure on the grass beside the pool.

'I've never seen the like,' an older gentleman said. 'He went down like a boulder.'

'I couldn't hold him up,' Halfpenny said. 'I swear his weight had doubled.'

'Negative buoyancy,' said the third man, rather younger than the other two. 'I've read about it but never seen it for myself. Quite remarkable.'

'You speak as if I were not here!' Watt said, sitting up and coughing.

'I thought you would drown, Watt. You simply sank before my eyes.'

'Yes,' Watt said, 'the same thought occurred to me. I remember now why I gave up trying to learn to swim when I was a boy.'

'Did this happen every time?'

'Yes. It tended to alarm people even more then.'

While they had been speaking, a small boy had wandered over wrapped in a towel. He was a pale lad, thin of arm and leg. He looked nervously from one to the other.

'Excuse me, but I am looking for Doctor Halfpenny,' he said.

'I am he,' Halfpenny told him.

'I am Oliver, Sir. Miss Hurst sent me to see you.'

Halfpenny looked puzzled for a few moments, then remembered. 'Oliver! Yes, I remember now. Gwendolyn–Miss Hurst–said you wanted to learn to swim, is that correct?'

'Yes, Sir,' the boy said without enthusiasm. He looked warily towards the pool, holding his towel tightly around him.

'Please continue without me,' Watt said. 'I shall rest for a moment. I may be a lost cause to swimming.'

'Well, Oliver, we shall make a start then,' Halfpenny said. 'Have you swum very much before?'

'No, Sir,' the boy said. 'I do not like the water on my face.'

'That's nothing to worry about, Oliver. You will soon become more confident,' Halfpenny told him.

'I don't think so, Sir,' Oliver said, 'but I will try.'

The boy moved hesitantly towards the pool steps. 'You will not plunge me in, Sir? Or push me suddenly?'

'No indeed,' Halfpenny said. 'You may rest assured of that.'

'My last swimming teacher believed in plunging people in,' Oliver said, stopping at the edge and frowning at the water lapping his toes.

'I once had a teacher with the same philosophy, Oliver,' Watt remarked. 'It was something I did not care for either.'

'Just step in now, Oliver. That is the shallow end. It will not come above your chest,' Halfpenny told his new pupil. But the boy seemed unable to move.

Halfpenny and Watt exchanged glances. 'Would you consider returning to the water, Theo? It might encourage the boy,' Halfpenny said. 'With your example, he might feel a little braver.'

'Not,' Watt said, aside, 'not if I sink and drown before his very eyes.'

'That can be avoided. I am sure of it.'

Watt sighed, but stood and joined Oliver at the pool steps. 'I think, if we cling to this bar at the side, and go in very slowly, we might, perhaps, both survive.'

'Can you not swim either, Sir?' Oliver seemed surprised.

'No. I sink.' Watt told him. He took the first two steps into the pool and reached for the bar.

'Perhaps I shall sink too.'

'Hold on here. Halfpenny will pull us out in case of disaster, won't you, Halfpenny? Halfpenny swims like a dolphin. He may actually *be* a dolphin.'

This made the boy smile. The two pupils edged slowly into the water, their knuckles white as they held onto the bar for dear life, and very slowly the swimming lesson began.

Chapter Ten

Hanks, smart in her best uniform, rolled her eyes in what he interpreted as a warning before she even took his hat. In the drawing room, he found his mother devoting her attention to an older couple. The lady wore an outfit foaming with lace and frills; her husband sat stiff as a punt pole on the sofa beside her. This gentleman seemed generally displeased and irritable, glaring about him making an occasional sound like 'chuh!' under his breath.

In the corner armchair, rarely chosen by guests because it was so out of the way, sat Miss Tatiana, for this was the McReedy-Roberts family. Miss Tatiana had the look of someone who had spent an uncomfortable morning at the hairdresser and an even more uncomfortable afternoon being fitted into her dress. She, too, was copiously frilled. Everything from her boots upward seemed too tight.

The professor was introduced by his Mama. Mrs McReedy-Roberts smiled and smiled. '*Enchantée*, my dear Professor! I have heard so much about you from your Mama,' she cried. 'You must tell Tatiana all about your work. She adores fish! Do you not, Tatiana? Trout! Haddock! Tatiana is entirely fascinated. Are you not, my dear?'

'Um, yes,' her daughter agreed without conviction.

Mr McReedy-Roberts took Theo's hand in a cold, harsh grip. 'I am a lawyer, Sir,' he said, by way of introduction. 'Is that clear?'

The rest of the company—they were fourteen in all—were old Cambridge friends and neighbours, mostly of his mother's generation. These were easy company because Theo had grown up among them. His academic distinction meant less to them than remembering the time Miss Pasterton caught him, aged eight, helping himself to pears from her favourite tree, or his early unsuccessful attempts at taxidermy. This cheerful group was no more eccentric than most groups of Cambridge neighbours, but it was easy to forget that visitors from elsewhere might not be accustomed to the oddities of academic life. His mother's next-door neighbour, Dr Jameson, for example, was a physicist and explosives expert and so was his Dutch wife. They were known for detonating experimental charges in the shed they had constructed for the purpose in their back garden. 'No need to worry, it's just the Jamesons,' people in Grange Road were used to saying when a volcano seemed to be exploding nearby.

Dr Bulimore, a medieval scholar and a fine lutanist, believed in cold water cures and had rigged up a mechanism in his garden for dousing himself twice a day. The cold water made him bellow and roar, but the neighbours were no longer worried.

Cheery conversation with this group passed the first few minutes, but Theo knew his duty was to break the ice with his mother's guest, so he went over.

'Do you know Cambridge well, Miss McReedy-Roberts?'

'Um no,' she said. 'We have been once before, but it rained.'

'Well, I gather we can expect sunshine for the next few days.'

'Um yes.'

'Why not take Tatiana into the garden, Theo? I'm sure she would like to see the pond, and the honeysuckle is very pleasant in the evening,' called his Mama. A general smile passed among the company. It was not possible to refuse.

In the garden a blackbird sang his last tune and a balmy scented cool had settled after the day's heat. Miss McReedy-Roberts stepped warily across the terrace, seeming unwilling to leave it and tread on the lawn.

'The path is dry, Miss…'

'Um, you may call me Tatiana,' she said.

'… Tatiana. The path is perfectly dry and safe.'

She stopped short on the steps. 'Insects,' she said. 'I cannot. Um, they do not agree with me.'

'You fear them?'

'Um, all buzzing things, yes. Disgusting!' She flicked something away from her face. 'Revolting things!' She now flapped both hands.

Theo had seen no insects, but the bats were coming out, so he reasoned there must be some. Tatiana saw the same thing. 'What is that?' she demanded, as a dark shape flitted over the pond.

'A bat. We have several species here. That is a horseshoe bat, so called because…'

'Eurgh! Get it away!' She held her arms over her head now, ready to protect herself.

'There is not the slightest need to concern yourself.'

'It will get into my hair!'

'No, not at all. It is afraid of you. They never come close enough to…'

But even as he spoke, there was a rustle in the branch of the walnut tree they stood under, and a black shape tumbled out and fell at Tatiana's feet. Its wings were spread, and it began to pull itself shakily across the paving.

'Get it away! Get it away!' Tatiana cried. 'Kill it! Stamp on it! I will not have it near me!'

'It is entirely harmless. It may have disoriented itself. Believe me, it cannot harm you!'

'Help! Help! It is coming closer! It will bite me. The dirty horrible thing will…' she was cringing with her eyes tightly closed and her fisted hands over her head.

'Tatiana! There is nothing to fear! Look!' he said. He bent and cautiously picked the animal up, folding its wings and holding them as he turned it over to examine it.

She opened one eye. He held it towards her, so that she could see how perfectly harmless, and indeed how small and delicate the little animal really was. She shrieked loudly and began gasping as if the breath had been knocked out of her.

'By Gad! What is happening out here?' The voice of Mr McReedy-Roberts echoed around the trees. He rushed across the terrace, followed by two other gentlemen, all greatly alarmed.

'Papa! It is a *creature*! Help me, please!' sobbed his trembling daughter.

'What has happened to you?' he shouted, outraged.

'It is nothing,' Theo explained. 'A bat merely.'

'A bat? What do you mean by frightening my daughter with a bat?'

'I had no intention of frightening her.'

'You wave an animal like a bat in the face of a young

lady and you do not expect her to be frightened? Are you mad, Sir?'

'It went for me, Papa!'

'It did no such thing.'

'It was tangled in my hair.'

'It was not!'

'Come Tatiana. Inside.'

Theo was left to release the bat by tossing it gently into the air. The other two gentlemen looked on.

'Not a country girl, I fear,' Dr Woolf finally declared. And after watching the bats swoop and twist in the dusk for a few moments more, they all went in to dinner.

Tatiana, revived by the doting sympathy of her hostess and parents, managed to eat a substantial dinner, but spoke not another word to Theo. He therefore passed the meal in conversation with his other table neighbour, Miss Munro, a lady well over eighty, who told him that she herself had never believed in marriage and advised him to avoid it, too, if he could. He might, she remarked, keep a cockatoo if he felt lonely. Cockatoos were excellent company.

If it came to a choice between Tatiana McReedy-Roberts and a cockatoo, he thought, on the walk back to Trinity, a cockatoo would certainly be his choice.

Chapter Eleven

'Miss McCreedy-Roberts will be free at noon tomorrow', his mother had told him, after the other guests had left.

'Is there any need to tell me that?' he asked. 'You saw how unmatched we were. She refused to address a word to me over dinner.'

'Theo. I have spoken to you before about the need to sustain an acquaintance for a period of time before one jumps to conclusions.'

'No, Mama. I must put my foot down. Tatiana is not someone I wish to acquaint myself with any further. She cannot abide insects and she actually urged me to stamp on a bat.'

'Tatiana has yet to be introduced to the wonders of nature, Theodore. She lives in Bury St Edmunds. A young town dweller cannot be expected to understand bats.'

Unaware of the misunderstanding over bats the night before, Lucia Venables was on high alert the following day for the arrival of Miss McCreedy-Roberts in the shop. Her plan to ensure a further meeting between this lady and Professor Watt was to have the lady and her mother encounter him on his afternoon walk, then to arrange for a pony cart and driver to pass conveniently along the Backs, ready to be engaged for a delightful ride. The driver had been paid to pass up and down the Backs for as long as necessary, which took some persuasion, though he agreed quickly enough when half-a-crown was mentioned. Since there were only two seats in the little pony trap, Lucia rested her hopes on Tatiana's mother deciding to leave the younger people to take the outing on their own.

Hummingbirds, however, interfered with this plan. Tatiana was entranced by them.

'I say! Mama, just look at the divine little bird on this straw. Who could resist?' She was turning her head and admiring herself in the looking glass before she had been inside the shop for two minutes.

'That is our newest range,' Christabel said. 'Hummingbirds are the talk of Paris this season.'

'Are they?' Tatiana was entranced by the glass. 'Can I carry it off, Mama?'

'Of course, my dear. It is most becoming on you.'

Lucia, posing as another customer, was trying on a dark straw with cherries at the other looking glass, but looked across at Tatiana. 'It flatters the shape of your face wonderfully well, if you will excuse me saying so.'

'I thought so,' said Tatiana. 'I am lucky to have an oval face. Most hat shapes suit me.'

'You are also most fortunate in your complexion. Such fair skin sets any hat off to great advantage,' added Lucia.

'But so very delicate,' her mother put in. 'She must on no account expose it to the sun.'

'No indeed,' Lucia agreed. 'On a day like this, you will need your parasol as well as a wide brim.'

'I shall—no question of that,' Tatiana agreed.

'Do you know the city well?' Lucia asked, looking back at her own reflection.

'Not well, no, we are only occasional visitors.'

'You will have taken a little driving tour, no doubt? And seen the Botanical Gardens?'

'Neither, as it happens,' Tatiana's mother said.

'On a day like today it would be the perfect outing, if I may say so,' Lucia removed the dark straw and selected a prettily ribboned day bonnet.

'Really? We thought of visiting the colleges.'

'Personally, I would advise against that. It is so stifling and airless in town,' Lucia said. 'The styles are quite superb in this establishment,' she added in a stage whisper to Mrs McCreedy-Roberts, having looked around as if to make sure that the proprietor was out of earshot. 'It is far and away the leading hat shop for ladies in the city. There are others—they may appear grander—but I can assure you, anything from Ladoré will always make the very best impression. Many fashionable ladies prefer to come here rather than pay the extortionate prices of the London fashion houses.'

'I thought so, Mama,' Tatiana said. 'I have an eye for quality, as you know.'

'I have always said that you had instinctively good taste,' her mother remarked. 'Ours is an artistic family.'

Tatiana tried three or four straws and boaters before returning to the original with its hummingbird. 'I cannot resist, Mama. I suppose my clothing allowance would stretch to it?'

'It would, though it might be better to spare your Papa the details.'

Tatiana giggled. 'I shall wear it. Put the old one in a box.'

'I should be delighted to show you to the Backs. It is a short stroll from here, and a delightful pony and trap is easily found there. You can take a drive in the cool under the trees almost as far as the Botanical Gardens.'

Mrs McReedy-Roberts handed her card to Christabel. 'Send the old hat to this address along with the account, if you please.' Her daughter was still admiring the new headgear from all angles. 'Shall we explore the Botanical Gardens, dear? They sound delightful.'

'They are out of town, one imagines,' Tatiana said, without taking her eyes from the looking glass.

'Not really. They are between here and the station. It is no distance,' Lucia said.

'I prefer the town,' Tatiana declared. 'Trees and lawns and flowerbeds—these are not the best places to show ones finest outfit to its best advantage. There will be nobody about. At least in the colleges, one might run across the sort of person who knows a fine hat when they see one.'

And they swept out of the door and away towards Magdalen College, where Lucia doubted very much that anyone would notice a hat at all. She looked at her watch. The timing would have been perfect. The professor would be strolling towards the Backs in five minutes.

'Ah well,' her sister said. 'I am no expert in matters of the heart, Lucia, as you know, but somehow I doubt Tatiana would make a soulmate for a professor, even if she does have very good taste in millinery.'

The doorbell rang and Ida Moss stepped into the shop with four new hummingbird hat decorations to deliver.

'Excellent. I have just sold the blue one,' Christabel told her. 'The wearer is parading it about town even as we speak.' She opened the till to pay Ida for her work.

'Will you need more birds?' Ida asked.

'Oh yes. At least four more. Can you manage that? And all different, as before. My clients love their hats to be unique in a few tiny details. The birds might have longer tail feathers or coloured beaks, for example.'

'And any colours in particular?' Ida asked.

'Green and blue are both popular. They are very skilfully made, Miss Moss. And how is the ancient jig-saw puzzle going?' Christabel asked. 'Ida's work is to piece together ancient and crumbling pieces of manuscript,' she explained to Lucia. Lucia looked up from her notebook.

'It is fascinating work,' Ida said. 'I am grateful for the reference.'

'I only told Mrs McAdam you were nimble-fingered and reliable. It was she who told me you were an expert in several languages. You are a dark horse, Ida.'

'Not an expert. But I was studying–before.'

Lucia interrupted. She was hastily preparing to leave. 'I am not admitting defeat yet. I shall go after Tatiana and her mother. I might be able to persuade them to a later 'accidental' meeting. But first I must hurry and dismiss the driver on the Backs or he will charge me again.'

'You will lose sight of the ladies if you do that first,' Christabel said. 'I cannot leave the shop, but perhaps Miss Moss would not mind sending the driver on his way?'

As she said this, she slid an extra coin into the row she had counted out to pay Ida.

'Of course,' Ida said. Gathering the coins into her

purse, she followed Lucia out of the shop. 'How will I know which driver to speak to?'

'The one with the neat little black cart. It has a striped sunshade,' Lucia said. 'I have paid in advance. Just tell him he is no longer needed, but please hurry, Ida, he is after another fee.'

Chapter Twelve

It was a warm day for hurrying through streets already baked in the sun for several hours. Ida chose the shady side of St John's Street, but even there the cobbles radiated heat and every unpleasant smell seemed to crowd the freshness out of the breezeless and humid atmosphere. Rain clouds, hazy and high, were gathering in the distance over the towers of Trinity as she approached.

Ida had her head down and did not see the bicycle. She stepped into Moat Lane as he pedalled out. His machine hit her only a glancing blow, but it threw her to the ground. He dismounted and ran back immediately, alarmed.

'I did not see you, Miss. Are you hurt? Shall I call for help?'

A passing lady and gentleman hurried over. The lady helped Ida to her feet.

'It is highly dangerous to cycle at speed in this manner!' The man told the cyclist. 'I have a good mind to call a policeman. You young men hurl yourselves about on these machines without a thought! You might have seriously injured this lady, or any other pedestrian!'

Several other passers-by arrived. A concerned circle formed on the pavement. Ida was sat on a chair brought from the nearest shop and passed a glass of water.

'It should be against the law,' someone declared. 'There is not enough space on the public highway for dangerous contraptions like bicycles!'

'The speed they go at!'

'They frighten the horses!'

'At least you can hear a horse coming. These bicycles can creep up on you from behind. It's a disgrace!'

The subject of this indignation was struggling to make it plain that she was perfectly unhurt. The dangers of bicycles had so inflamed the group in the street that few of them heard this. She stood and looked for someone to thank, but nobody paid her any attention until she cleared her throat loudly.

'I am not harmed! Thank you all for your assistance.'

'Shall I call you a cab?' someone asked.

'No, thank you. I shall just make my way now.'

The crowd was collectively unsure that this was wise.

'I know this lady. I shall accompany her,' a man's voice said beside her. With a bow, professor Watt tipped his hat, took Ida's arm and walked her away.

'I trust you really are unhurt,' he said, after a few steps.

'I am perfectly undamaged, but I have been delayed,' she said. 'I am on an errand.'

'I shall accompany you, in that case. For safety's sake. In case you suffer a delayed reaction. Delayed reactions—shock and so on—they can be unpredictable.'

'Are you knowledgeable in medical matters?'

'No. Not at all. I dislike medical matters as a general

rule, but my mother is a great expert, and she always warns against delayed reactions. She probably has a cousin who collapsed an hour after seeming unhurt in a street accident. My mother can usually find an illustrative example from among her friends and family.'

This made Ida smile.

'I must get to the Backs to send a cart driver on his way.'

'Then that is where we shall go.'

'I can walk without assistance,' Ida told him.

He did not release her hand. He had tucked it under his elbow and he continued to hold it there. 'Unless you absolutely forbid it, Miss Moss, I feel it would be safer for me to continue to steady you.'

'In case of a sudden collapse?'

'Exactly so.'

They walked on. The street leading to the bridge was narrow and shady. The heat here diffused by the river. Punts passed, the voices of the passengers echoing as they passed under the bridge. Neither Ida nor the professor spoke for a while, enjoying the quiet sounds of lapping water and people on a boat trip.

'Do you punt, Miss Moss?' he asked, eventually.

'I? No. I have never tried.'

'Nor even been a passenger in one?'

'Not even a passenger, no.'

'And you have lived in Cambridge for... how long?'

'Four years now.'

'Four years and never been in a punt! That must be remedied.'

'Perhaps one day.'

'A picnic is usually recommended.'

'I shall bear that in mind.'

They had crossed the bridge. The Backs were in sight.

'I am to tell the driver of the neat black cart with the striped awning that he need not wait.'

They both looked up and down. No carts were in sight. Clouds were gathering and beginning to darkening.

'There is no need for you to wait, Professor. I am perfectly well.'

'You *think* you are well, but I could not live with myself if you suffered, for example, a sudden seizure. Another bicycle might crash into you. A horse might bolt.'

'I have no further need of your protection.'

'I was only being light-hearted, Ida,' he said. He let go of her arm and looked down at his feet. 'In truth, I am the one who needs protecting.'

'And what could you need protection from?'

He continued to look at the ground. A few rain drops were beginning to fall. 'From my books. From spending another afternoon at my desk re-arranging the semi-colons in my manuscript. From my mother's plans.'

A small cart approached from the direction of Castle Hill. Its awning was striped. It slowed in front of them.

'For the Botanical Gardens?' the driver asked, pulling the pony up. It was a pretty piebald animal. It flicked its black tail and turned to look at them between its blinkers.

Ida was about to speak, but Watt took her arm again. 'Please come for a drive, Miss Moss. Rescue me, please?'

A sudden shower was close. The driver drew the awning up and over the seat and fastened an oilskin cover in front, almost up to their chins. And then the heavens opened. Rain clattered on the roof and beat on either side. Even under the shelter of the trees, the pony and driver were drenched. Giant raindrops bounced and splattered the road. An instant flood soon coursed in every gutter. Along the paths, hurrying pedestrians held dripping parasols, newspapers or the shoulders of their jackets over their heads and huddled in the cover of the great lime trees, but the first clap of thunder sent most dashing out for fear of lightning strikes.

'I cannot move him, Sir,' the driver called from his seat ahead. 'Not in this. We shall have to wait until it passes.'

'No hurry, driver,' the professor called back.

It was exhilarating, this summer storm. He wondered if she felt it, too. Ida was looking at a group of boys too wet now to care, dancing and chasing one another through puddles, calling and splashing in delight.

'You are dry enough, Miss Moss?' he asked.

She turned a face towards him that he couldn't read. Her eyes were dark blue, he saw, and her nose was a little freckled. Her mouth...

'Perfectly dry, thank you,' she said. 'I find myself envying those foolish boys.'

Theo looked. 'They will catch their death of cold, if my mother is to be believed.'

'Most mothers would say the same. But they are not always right,' she said, still watching the children splash about.

'Do you mean to imply, Miss Moss, that sometimes people take risks and no harm whatever results?'

She laughed and turned to look at him again. 'It is a dangerous thought, but yes, I do.'

'How is your work at the library?'

'I have already talked at length about it. Probably too much at length. I was embarrassed when I realised how much I chattered the other day. It was the excitement of a new discovery.'

'Of course, but I enjoyed hearing you speak of it.'

'I feel so very fortunate. I have not been able to carry out any meaningful work for a long time. And what of you, Professor? What of ichthyology?'

Her mouth, he thought, had the most perfect shape. Especially when she said the word *'ichthyology'*. You could carve her in marble and she would outshine any goddess in the classical archaeology department. They would be marble, and she living and warm.

'Professor?' she prompted. The rain drummed on the canvas roof of the carriage.

He smiled. 'Ah yes, ichthyology. It goes well. I am working at present on a particular group of fossils. I specialise in the front fins. It is the bones of the front fins, you see, that indicate the exact stage of development each species has reached. The German fossils I am recording at present...'

After a few minutes the rainstorm moved away, the horse shook himself thoroughly, and the driver asked them if they were ready to go.

Watt turned to Ida. 'We can hardly dismiss the poor man after he has given us shelter. The least we can do is to give him a fare and a decent tip when we get there.'

'I can walk home from the Botanical Gardens,' she said. 'It is not too far.'

The driver flicked the reins, and they pulled away.

'But I hope you will walk in the gardens with me for a few minutes beforehand?' Watt asked. 'The roses may have passed their best, but there will be plenty to see. If we avoid the trees, we should not be too much dripped on.'

Ida looked uncomfortable. 'Professor,' she said, 'it is a little irregular.'

'What is irregular, Miss Moss?'

'For us to be seen together—an unaccompanied single lady and a gentleman—in public.'

'Do you concern yourself with such things?' He looked at her. The question was genuine.

'I? Oh, Professor, I am far beyond worrying about what the gossips of Cambridge, or anywhere else have to say about *me*! No, I was thinking of you. A university man. A distinguished one. You must have a reputation to consider.'

'Ah,' he said, 'I see. Well, if I were to misidentify the metacarpal bone of a Celocamp, there might be consequences, but riding in a carriage with a lady conservator of manuscripts presents, I think, very little risk.'

They were well under way, crossing Silver Street, the pony and the meadows both steaming as the heat of the afternoon returned.

'Conservator is putting it a bit high,' she remarked. And she turned aside so that only the cattle grazing the long grass saw the thrill of pleasure his answer gave her.

Chapter Thirteen

There are times in Cambridge—perhaps in every city—when each stone and tree, each building and cobble and archway and tower, each climbing rose and lawn and gate and ancient doorway conspires to create a portrait of unforgettable perfection. Visitors to the city on such a day leave with a memory that glows untarnished in their heart for decades.

It is wisest not to return in case the city's eternal beauty is not quite at her best a second time; '*by chance or nature's changing course untrimm'd,*' as the poet says.

Susceptibility to this powerful loveliness is likely to be amplified in hearts experiencing tender feelings. Both the people strolling in the Botanical Gardens that afternoon lived in Cambridge and ought, otherwise, to have a certain immunity to her charms. But that day they had none. The glorious gardens, the sun returning to a clear sky, the atmosphere refreshed by the sudden storm; all together put on a display that hearts far harder than those of the Professor and Miss Moss could resist as they strolled the paths between flowerbeds and examined the cactuses and ferns in the greenhouses.

Several elements of this walk took Watt by surprise. Their conversation, for one thing. He generally found talking to young women very hard work. *Making* conversation often felt like *making* a cake or *making* a shoe—something requiring a good deal of expertise and concentration that he did not have. Long silences would fall with both parties searching their ideas for something to say, the way bridge players with a losing hand scour their cards for even a weak one to put down. Or, even worse, the lady in question would not stop talking. He had sat at dinner beside young women who seemed to be able to speak without drawing breath for two hours at a time. They could eat with perfect manners, whilst talking continuously. It felt to Watt like being suffocated by a scented cushion.

Conversation with Miss Moss was as easy as breathing the summer air. No effort of any sort was required. Words—thoughts—flowed limpidly between them. They laughed together, they spoke of any topic that came to mind without, it seemed to him, any hesitation, pretence, display or hiding on either part. Such easy amiability with a young woman he knew only a little was something he had only dimly imagined might even be possible. And here it was. Here *she* was, stepping over puddles on the gravel path of a green-dappled avenue at his side.

He had asked about her father.

'He was an engineer,' she said. 'On the railways. A very proud engineer. Over a cup of tea, he will tell anyone the lines he had a hand in planning. He is retired from that now and mostly does welfare work for the union.'

'How did you come to live here? You said you came four years ago, but from where?'

'From London. We wanted a change. My father retired, so we looked for somewhere—well, to be honest, we looked for a backwater. Somewhere very quiet.'

'Oh dear, a backwater. But, yes, I suppose Cambridge is an odd place.'

'I meant no insult to the great university. Only that the city is small and people come and go. That suited us, I suppose. And the union could find us a railway house. One that was tucked away.'

'And what do you make of the city yourself?'

'I like it. Our circumstances have sometimes been difficult, but the colleges and the old streets are delightful. And having work at the University Library—that will be a great help.'

He so hated the idea of this little woman, plainly enough dressed but outshining every blossom they passed, enduring any sort of difficulty at all that he lost concentration and almost tripped over the tidy edging of the lawn.

'Do you mind my asking how you were educated?' he asked. 'I mention it because I had a strange education myself. I did not go to school because of my health. I had tutors. They were chosen by my father at first, and later by my Mama, who mainly judged according to their fees, I think. They were an interesting, but eccentric collection.'

'Were you ill for a long time?'

'Yes. Weakness of the chest. Bronchitis every year and so on.'

'How horrid.'

'I grew stronger as I grew older, but it left my mother rather set in her habits of over-protection.'

'She worries. That is only natural. You are her only son?'

'Her only child. And you, Miss Moss? Do you have a brother or sister?'

She paused and looked across the grass towards the ornamental pond. 'I did have a sister, but she is no longer with us.'

'I'm so sorry. I hope it is not a recent loss?'

'Five years ago now. We still miss her terribly.'

He could hardly bear her distress. It made him momentarily frantic. 'We were talking of education,' he prompted, hoping to distract her.

'Yes,' she said. To his pleasure, her face regained a little of its bloom. 'Education. Well, my father is a great believer in education. He sent us to school as soon as we could walk and hold a piece of chalk. There was a school nearby, and a good one. Training teachers came there, our lessons were their experiments. Both of us learnt everything they offered. We won scholarships later. Mine was to study languages. My sister was extremely good at mathematics. She had a special prize and could study in Belgium at the university in Louvain because of it.'

'That is most impressive.'

'My father brought us up to believe that you can learn anything at all if you only find the right library books.'

'He is right, of course,' Watt said, 'though a certain amount of diligent study is needed as well.'

'He supplied the library books; we supplied the hard work.'

'He must be very proud of you both.'

She had been smiling, but this made her serious again. They were close to the pond. She stood at the edge and looked into it. A trio of carp changed course and swam across to look up at her, hoping for food.

'He is, I think,' she said. 'But, professor, he will also be waiting for me, and wondering where I am. I have enjoyed this afternoon. Thank you, but now I must leave you and make my way home.'

He hated this sudden change in her. 'Allow me at least to walk you to the gate,' he said.

But she shook her head, turned on her heel, and followed the curving path away.

Theo looked down at the pond. The fish were now under a lily pad. 'I still owe that lady a farthing,' he told them.

Chapter Fourteen

The sun was blazing again as the next swimming lesson ended. The two beginners, one tall, one short, sat on the side of the pool with their legs in the water, glad to be warmed by its rays, and watched Halfpenny demonstrate the breaststroke.

'Your hands are together, you see,' he said. 'Push them forward like this, then pull back, and at the same time, kick like a frog at the back. You'll soon get it. Show me the arm movements.'

'It's all very well in theory,' Watt said, as he and Oliver imitated the arm movements in the air, 'but I never seem to get as far as a stroke of any kind. I just hit the bottom.'

Oliver, who was making progress so fast that he had lost all fear of having his face splashed and could even put his head under if he pinched his nose first, giggled beside him.

'Are you laughing at me, young man?'

'No, Sir. Sorry Sir,' he said. 'It is a real phenomenon. I looked it up.'

'Looked what up?'

Halfpenny had speeded up and was now swimming up and down with his head bobbing up for air in perfect rhythm with his arms. It seemed miraculous to Watt.

'Negative buoyancy, Sir. I looked it up in an encyclopaedia at the library.'

'Really?'

'Yes, Sir. It is something to do with the ratio of fat and muscle and bone. It is fat that has the least mass and therefore it floats most easily. Then comes muscle. If you don't have very much fat or much muscle, your body is more dense than the water and it cannot float.'

Oliver's summary of his physical deficiencies, though bald, was strangely comforting.

'It is not my doing then? There is nothing I can do about it?'

'Well, in the book it said you *might* learn to swim, but only with difficulty. Would you care for a toffee?' the boy asked suddenly, fearing perhaps that he might have caused offence. 'I have one in my pocket in the changing room.' He ran off to fetch it without waiting.

Halfpenny swam over and, panting as he leaned his chin on the edge of the pool, watched the boy go.

'He is a kind lad,' Watt remarked.

'It is a sad and difficult family situation,' Halfpenny said. 'Gwendolyn has told me something of it. She has taken them on as one of her good causes. By the way, Watt, I was going to ask a favour. Would you mind accompanying Gwendolyn and me as we walk the boy back to her house? His aunt is to meet him there. I need a few words with Gwen alone and opportunities are rare—her father's a stickler for a chaperone. You could occupy the boy—talk to him and so on. If you wouldn't mind.'

Oliver returned and sat again beside Watt, handing him

a toffee wrapped in waxed paper. 'Here you are, Sir,' he said.

'Very kind of you, Oliver. Can it be spared?'

'Yes. I have five more.'

Halfpenny plunged backwards and began demonstrating a vigorous front crawl. His pupils watched him, chewing.

The walk through town followed an extended and winding route chosen by Halfpenny to prolong conversation with Gwendolyn for as long as possible. It seemed to take in most of the city. They wandered through Green Street, back through Rose Crescent and the market and out across the Backs. Halfpenny and Gwendolyn soon drew ahead. Seeing them from a distance, the clear pleasure they took in each other's company was obvious, Watt thought.

Oliver, normally reserved, was talkative on the walk. His fair hair stuck out in all directions. He had buttoned his shirt wrongly and he did not know how to roll a towel, so began by carrying a damp bundle with trailing corners.

'May I help with that?' Watt asked after a while. 'So that you do not trip over it again?'

'Yes, please.'

Watt twisted some of the water out of the dripping bathing suit and rolled it inside the towel.

They strolled on through the afternoon streets.

'What is your favourite subject at school, Oliver?'

'I like mathematics,' he said. 'I keep up easily. I usually get nine out of ten. Sometimes ten.'

'Very good. Very good.'

'Did you have a best subject, Sir?'

They stood aside to allow an elegant carriage to pass. It

was unlike the more humble vehicles usually seen in Cambridge.

'I always liked Natural History, birds, botany, nature walks and so on. But I never went to school myself.'

This was a shocking idea to the boy. 'You did not go to school?'

'I was ill a lot of the time. I did have lessons. Tutors came to me.'

'All alone? Just you?'

'Yes. I was never in a class until I came to university. It was very strange then.'

'But you had friends to play with?'

'I had neighbours, and I played with visitors when I was well.'

The boy looked at the pavement as he walked, considering this for a moment.

'But now you are a professor and that means you are very clever,' he said.

'If you find something that truly interests you, it is a pleasure to learn about it. As you know from mathematics.'

'Yes,' said the boy, but added, 'you have to do other subjects for the scholarship, though. Latin and so on.'

'Is that more difficult?'

'Miss Hurst is helping me. She makes it as easy as she can. I already know *amo, amas, amat, amamus, amantis, amant.*' The sound of a carriage door slamming ahead made the boy look up.

Watt smiled, wondering for the first time why the verb 'to love' was nearly always the first thing taught in Latin lessons. He was about to ask the boy if he knew any other verbs, when he realised the child had gone from his side.

Watt scanned the street ahead, but there was no sign of him. He turned and looked the way they had come, but again, the child was not there. He looked into the shops on either side—a grocer's and a bookbinder's, but both were clearly empty. How could he have disappeared? Watt began to hurry back towards the market, but looking into a shadowy alleyway, he saw the outline of the child silhouetted against a side wall, lit by the sunlight at the other end. He appeared to be trying to hide.

Watt hurried over. 'Is this hide and seek? I thought you were lost!' he said, but the boy's face was white.

'Please Sir. Do not tell him.'

'Tell who?'

'That gentleman in the big carriage. Do not tell him I am here. Please.'

Watt bent to look at the boy. He was shivering and close to tears.

'What is this, Oliver?'

'Please Sir. The gentleman. I must not... He must not see me. Please.'

Whatever this was, the boy was genuine in his alarm. 'My college is nearby, Oliver. I shall take you inside. You will be quite safe. They will not let a stranger in. Follow me quickly. Stay close.'

They were at the Porter's Lodge in minutes. 'I shall be showing this young gentleman around the college and giving him tea in my rooms,' Watt told Bill. 'If Dr Halfpenny is looking for us, please direct him there.'

'Yes, Sir. Would you like a cake sent up?' The porter had shrewdly assessed the boy as needing something to steady him.

'Good idea. Yes please. In about a quarter of an hour.

Now, Oliver, you are perfectly safe here. Strangers cannot enter the college. That is so, isn't it, Bill?'

'No stranger gets past us here in the Porter's Lodge, Professor,' Bill said, standing tall in his bowler hat. He could see that the boy needed reassurance.

Watt led the boy around Great Court and into the dining hall, where Oliver stood open-mouthed with his head thrown back taking in the great height and the arched and spindled stalactites of the famous ceiling. Enormous portraits of copiously wigged college dignitaries peered back down at them. College servants were beginning to set a few of the tables.

'Is that King Henry VIII, Sir?' the boy asked recognising one of the figures.

They looked up at the famous portrait. Broad in his jewelled furs and velvets, Henry stood with his powerful stockinged legs planted well apart, glaring a cold-eyed challenge.

'It is. He founded the place. He has the legs of a strong cyclist, I always think. But a mean little mouth.' He was relieved to see that this made Oliver smile. The colour began to come back into his face.

After taking in the chapel and the fountain and stepping into the library, they climbed the winding stone stairs to Watt's rooms. A tea tray was waiting, along with a walnut cake.

'Are these books all yours, Sir?' The boy asked.

'Yes. All these.'

'Have you read all of them?'

Watt considered his answer. 'In truth, I have not read *all* of all of them, but I think I have certainly read part of almost every one. Except the novels. My mother occasionally gives me novels. They are in the corner there. I don't usually read them.'

'Do they have fairies? I do not like fairies in stories. Or mermaids.'

'Nor I.'

'Or chimney sweeps.'

'I'm with you there, Oliver.'

Footsteps suddenly came up the stairs and the door was flung open. Halfpenny, breathless, rushed in. 'There you are. Gwendolyn was worried, but I told her you would find your way here. Are you alright, Oliver?'

'Yes, thank you,' said the boy, around a mouthful of cake. He was looking out of the window, taking in the fine view of the court and the towers of the building beyond.

'Splendid work, Watt.'

'There is tea,' Watt said.

'We must hurry back to Gwendolyn. She is waiting with the boy's aunt. They have been terribly alarmed.' He gave Watt a look which discouraged further questions, but then took his arm and led him further from the child. 'He explained, I suppose?'

'No. He was suddenly afraid. I still have no idea why. Only that he saw someone—a gentleman—someone in a grand carriage.'

'I cannot explain now, I must restore him to his aunt. The Devereaux case, have you heard of it?'

'I may have heard the name, I'm not sure.' Watt did not know what to make of this.

'Look it up, Watt, the boy is connected. He is in danger. I'll explain at dinner.'

Chapter Fifteen

One of the foremost qualities of the experienced librarian is the ability to respond without reaction to a request of any sort. They share this level of restraint with the finest butlers and those who win at poker.

Dr Chapman, the librarian at Trinity, did not so much as blink when the Professor, whose usual requests were in Fossil Archeology or Natural History, suddenly wanted the archived press coverage of a notorious divorce scandal.

'I want to read about the Devereaux case. It was a well-known court case, I believe.'

'It was indeed,' said the librarian. 'It ran in the newspapers for a year or more.'

'How long ago?'

The librarian swivelled on his heel and ran his eyes down a column of small drawers before pulling one out and trotting his fingers over the packed index cards. 'Let me see. That would be five years ago, ah yes, 1890 to 91. We have the papers. They will be boxed in the periodicals room.'

'I need to see them,' Watt said.

'All of them?'

'Will there be a great many?'

'It was written about daily for a year, at least. The case caused something of a sensation at the time.'

Watt sighed. 'I would have been writing my thesis. I suppose I must have heard something about it.'

'It was a very notorious case. It attracted widespread reports.' The librarian consulted the notes on his card. 'It was written up in all the daily newspapers, but one magazine, the Pall Mall Gazette, summarised events weekly on a Saturday.'

'Perhaps you could seek out the Pall Mall gazette for that year, then?'

'Of course. There appears also to be a short pamphlet written by the lady at the centre of the scandal at the time. We have that too.'

'Thank you, that would be helpful.'

Watt settled himself at one of the tables among the carved shelves of the great library and opened his notebook. He was there long after the librarian had left. When the dinner bell rang, he left the piles of magazines, and with his back stiff after several hours' intense concentration, hurried away.

'You have read about the case already?' Halfpenny asked as soon as Grace had been said before dinner.

'I have. It is hard reading. What a dreadful set of events. Scarcely believable.'

A celery soup was placed in front of them.

'But Halfpenny, what has this scandal with every

deplorable detail raked over by the press and feasted on by a cruel public? What has this got to do with Oliver? I am still at a loss.'

'His name is Oliver Devereaux.'

Watt blinked and frowned over his soup dish, trying to take this in. 'Oliver is connected to this monster? This terrible man who lied and deceived and disgraced himself in court for all to see?'

'Oliver is his son, Watt.'

'Good God! You are surely not serious?'

'Completely serious.'

Watt was still unable to eat or look up from his plate. 'But how is he here? How did he come to be in Cambridge having swimming lessons, of all things?'

'His family is here in Cambridge now. They live very quietly. They are trying to do what they can for Oliver, but it isn't easy. They live in fear of the wretched father. He recently threatened to take the boy. Despite publicly disowning the child for many years, the wretch now seems to believe there would be some financial advantage to him if the boy were in his charge.'

'Surely he would not snatch the child in the street?'

'You have read the case, Watt. You can see for yourself. He will stop at nothing if he thinks it will give him the upper hand or cause the innocent people he thinks of as his enemies even more misery.'

'He must be deranged.'

'Perhaps he is,' Halfpenny said. 'But he is also wealthy enough to act with impunity. He has thumbed his nose at the courts for years.'

'Is it Gwendolyn who made these discoveries?'

'She has come to know the boy's aunt well. Ida Moss, her name is.'

Hearing that name brought Watt up short. '*Ida Moss?*'

'You know her?'

'Well, yes. Not very well, though, it seems.'

'She is Oliver's aunt. They live with her father in Cooper Street.'

The soup was taken from in front of Watt and replaced with a trout, its mouth open and its eyes fried white. Watt could only stare blindly back at it.

Hanks had a secretive look when he arrived at his mother's house the following day for tea, but it changed to one of concern as she took his hat.

'You look peaky, Master Theo. Not working too hard?'

'I am well enough, Hanks, thank you.'

'Tea will be in the garden. There is a visitor,' she said, but had gone before he could ask more.

From across the lawn, he could only see a second lady in conversation with his mother, but then he recognised a familiar face.

'Mary! Mary Tipton!'

'I wanted it to be a surprise, Theo!' the younger lady said, rising and holding out her hands to greet him. 'It's been such an age!'

'When did you return? I thought you had decided to stay on.'

She stepped back, smiling.

'I missed the old country. Cambridge in particular. And you, Theo? Your mother tells me your work is widely recognised now.'

'It goes well, thank you. How are you, Mary?'

'I was ill for a while in India. It weakens one's constitution. I have not been strong since. You, on the other hand, appear to be thriving. You have caught the sun.'

'I am learning to swim, believe it or not.'

'You didn't tell me,' said his mother. 'You do not swim in the river, I hope? Angelica Marshall's sister broke a leg only last year when she fell out of a punt!'

'I swim in the Fellows' pool at Emmanuel.'

'That is a good deal safer, I imagine. But you should avoid sitting in a wet bathing costume. The cold against the skin is very conducive to chills.'

'Well, when I say that I swim, I barely do. I can only just keep my head above water,' Watt said.

Mary laughed. He had forgotten Mary's laugh. It was candid and sudden. He had been partial to it, growing up.

'How did you think Mary looked?' his mother asked as he was leaving. A cab had called for Mary after a single cup of tea, and she had left for her friend's house at Madingley.

'She looked well, I thought.'

'She is thin.'

'A little.'

'Thin and drawn about the eyes. She was unwell for a long time after John died. Her health may be damaged permanently. And all alone out there, in a foreign country.'

'She knew a lot of people in the regiment, I expect.'

'Yes, but she was very far from home. So tragic to lose him that way.'

'Remind me. It was a fever?'

'Yes. Perfectly well and hearty one day, then a single day's fever, and he was dead by the evening. In a paroxysm. One can scarcely imagine the shock. Poor, dear Mary. And after only two years of marriage.'

'Yes. Poor Mary.'

'She was such a bonny girl when you were both young. Always laughing.'

'Yes, I remember.'

'You were fond of her, I think.'

'It was a very long time ago, Mama.'

'At my age, time is different. One moment your children are babies; the next they are *approaching middle age*,' his mother said, standing to walk him to the garden gate. 'Time waits for no man. Mary will be staying with her friends for several weeks, I believe. She would welcome the company of an old friend, I'm sure.'

'Thank you, Mama. But now I must get back to my work, before I am too ancient to hold a pen any longer.'

'The professor's mother has abandoned hope of the hummingbird hat lady, then?' Christabel said. She was stitching a ribbon onto a bonnet in the back room of the shop.

Lucia, reading her notebook, frowned. 'She was only interested in parading her new hummingbirds among the colleges. I spent half the afternoon following, but there was no herding the pair of them onto any path that would cross the professor's. They visited three tea shops in one afternoon to avoid the downpour. All I could do was to stand in three doorways, sheltering.'

'The Moth Agency's line of work may be more arduous than one imagined,' Christabel said, adding, 'Ow!' as the thimble slipped and she plunged the sewing needle into her finger.

'Hat selling has its dangers too, though,' Lucia said,

hiding a smile at her sister's irritation. 'There is the tedium, for one thing.'

'Nonsense! I have been rushed off my feet for weeks.'

'And the deceit…'

'What deceit?'

'Not telling Miss Kirby that she looks like a mushroom in that hat, or Mrs Fullerton that a very heavy veil might help her looks, but little else would.'

'That is professional tact, it is not deception.'

'Tact is very overrated, in my opinion.'

'It never was a strength of *yours*, certainly. The professor's mother has not yet given up hope, though?'

'There is a new candidate. Much nearer the mark, by the sound of her. An old friend. She was re-introduced to the professor at dinner last night, and today I may be required to arrange another coincidental meeting. Mrs Watt is calling to let me know.'

'Feel free to use my shop as a meeting place,' Christabel said.

'They buy hats! Why should you object? I may dispense with my own office entirely.'

Her sister had opened her mouth to argue, but the doorbell rang and Mrs Watt bustled in. 'Now Lucia, good news!' she said. 'My son has at last taken the initiative and invited the lady in question out himself. It was touch and go. He only did so only on the very threshold, as she was putting on her coat to leave. I may have nudged him slightly. Anyway, they are to meet today. Your services will not be needed.' Her eyes wandered at this point over the hats displayed on their stands around the shop. Christabel had a talent for arranging her creations. 'I have a little time on my hands. I might, perhaps, take a moment to investigate your sister's marvellous range. Something for chapel during the Michaelmas Term.'

'And perhaps even for a wedding?' Christabel suggested.

Mrs Professor Watt beamed, as she untied her own bonnet and took a seat before one of the mirrors. 'We must not count our chickens, but, yes, who knows?'

Chapter Sixteen

Mary was waiting at the gate to the Fellow's Garden when Theo arrived. A stroll there had been her choice.

'What I have longed for and missed more than anything is a college garden, Theo. There are delightful gardens in Darjeeling, but the plants are so different. I should love above all to wander somewhere supremely lush and green. A Cambridge garden lovingly tended for several hundred years.'

'That is easily done,' he had said.

She was looking away as he approached. Her tall figure turned towards Queens College was familiar, but also changed. She was, as his mother had said, thinner. The shoulder he could see in outline was an angle, the jaw under the bonnet, sharp. But she smiled warmly and stepped towards him as he approached under the trees, and was restored to the younger Mary he had known. A playful child, bringing stories and make-believe games to his sick room; an energetic school girl, who loved gossip and giggled with him about the awfulness of teachers. A poised young woman, swept into a whirl of parties and dances and falling in love with the handsome military son of a judge. Was he jealous, he wondered, as he opened the gate and led her into the garden, through a tunnel of leaves. Had it been a mistake to let this Mary, his familiar friend, marry another man and disappear?

'You are thoughtful, Theo,' she said. 'Is something troubling you? Perhaps you cannot really spare the time to walk the gardens. Your fossils call to you, no doubt!'

'It is a call I can easily resist in favour of a summer's afternoon with you, Mary.'

This made her smile. 'I thought of you often when I was away. You were a sort of touchstone for me. It sounds odd, but I often used you, or the idea of you, to judge new people I met.'

'I would make a poor yardstick,' he said. 'Most of them would have been taller than me, at a guess.'

'You were a very good yardstick, as it happens. If they were not as kind as you, I knew I should not like them; if they were, I knew I should.'

'You flatter me.'

'Why should I do that? You are the very kindest person I have ever met. You were even as a boy.'

'Kind?' he said.

'Yes. I can remember you going to great lengths to rescue butterflies that flew against windows, birds caught in the fruit netting, even spiders threatened by Hanks's broom!'

'Hanks has always hated spiders,' he said. 'I had to be quick!'

'My brothers stamped on spiders. My sisters screamed and hit them with a newspaper.'

'I am definitely kind to spiders, but that is an odd yardstick to measure people by.'

'Most men I met were not as kind. Most women were not, either, come to that. Shall we sit for a while?'

They settled on a bench which looked along the broad curve of a lawn. Behind them a curtain of weeping willow, which rustled in the idle breeze.

Theo turned to look at his childhood friend. She was at ease now, a smile on her face as she looked around them at the perfectly tended garden, but her eyes, he thought, still held sadness. 'It has been a hard few years for you, Mary.'

'Do you say that because my looks are so altered?' The question surprised and unsettled him. 'Come now, Theo, we both know this is true.'

'We are both a little older,' he began.

'I look worn and tired. I look like someone who has had a long illness. I see my own face every day. I am under no illusion.'

People had begun crossing the lawn on the far side from another entrance, three or four at a time. Some had their arms full of clothing, others held hats or carried chairs or benches. They all headed purposefully towards a corner of the garden screened by shrubs and trees. Theo watched them without attention. The tone of defeat in Mary's voice confused him. Mary did not fish for compliments. She meant this, and she was right. He did not know what to say.

'I have changed,' Mary said. 'Outwardly and inwardly. In so many years, one would expect it. But it is good to see that you have not changed. You are still the same kind Theo. Still delighting in the natural world, studying it, writing about it, discovering new things about it. Still my steady touchstone.'

They began to hear sounds from the far end of the garden. Instruments appeared to be tuning up. Even more people were crossing the lawn now. Mary smiled suddenly.

'They must be putting on a play, Theo. Shall we go and see?'

'Yes, why not? What will it be, do you think?'

They watched the last few actors hurrying across the lawn. One had a painted lion's mask, another a pair of donkey's ears.

'The Dream!' they said together.

'How many times have we sat on the damp grass and watched this play?' he asked.

'Oh, it must be half a dozen times, at least. I was a fairy once, remember? I was about four years old. I wore a gauzy skirt and a hat like a carrot top.'

'What were your lines?'

'No lines. I had to skip prettily on and off and remember to follow the Fairy Queen. I found it all terribly dull and fell asleep on stage, but nobody noticed.'

'I remember the Master playing Oberon once. He had to be prompted for almost every line.'

'That was the year the Bellini twins played Helena and Hermia. Do you remember? Our mothers were outraged by their costumes. They were filmy and short. There was a great deal of leg on display.'

'They were rather splendid girls. I certainly remember that.'

'Every undergraduate at the university remembers the Bellinis!'

'Did you never feel like acting, Mary? You know the play well enough.'

'No. I reached my peak as an actress as a sleepy fairy at the age of four. Did you consider it yourself?'

'Not for a second.'

'I have always admired your lack of vanity, Theo. It is a fine quality.'

'I lack talent. I can be vain.'

'Can you? What is your vanity?'

'I am vain about my work. I believe it to be more important and far, far more interesting than almost everyone else's. I have only recently begun to reconsider that. What vanities have you, Mary, if any?'

She looked towards the stage. Props were being arranged and a man wearing a doublet and hose was tuning a guitar.

'I am vain enough to believe my judgement of people is rather sound. My ability to discern people's state of mind and their character. I am convinced of my unusual perceptive abilities in that area. I may be completely deluded, of course, but I don't think so. Why have you recently begun to reconsider the importance of your work?'

'I met some people whose worlds are different.'

'Yes, that would do it. Who, in particular?'

'Someone who has had a difficult past.'

'You know this person well?'

'I thought I was beginning to, but I discovered I did not.'

'They kept things from you? You felt deceived?'

'I felt distrusted. Excluded.'

'That upset you a great deal?'

'It did. More than I expected.'

'This person, was their past so difficult that it might have damaged their ability to trust people?'

'Definitely.'

'Then you can hardly have expected them to share their secrets. I presume you have not known this person for long?'

'Not long, no.'

'And your discovery has disturbed you?'

'It has.'

'Quite profoundly?'

'Yes, indeed.'

'Why?'

'I beg your pardon?'

'Why are you so disturbed by discovering something about the past of a person, you know only a little?'

'I thought I had more of her trust.'

'Is it her own behaviour in the past that is at fault?'

'No. She has done nothing wrong.'

'They why judge her so harshly?'

'I do not!'

'Are you in love with her, Theo?'

'No! We have spoken on only two or three occasions. We rescued a fish.'

'You rescued a fish! Together?'

'Yes. A chub.'

'Ah! *A chub*,' Mary said, looking towards the stage. 'The species of fish would make all the difference, obviously.'

The music struck up, and with the audience gathered around them on the grass, the play began.

Chapter Seventeen

Later, as they left the garden, Mary said. 'Your Mama once had hopes of us, I think. Hopes of us making a pair, I mean. She may have them again now.'

Theo sighed. She was holding his arm, and he patted her hand at his elbow. 'She was always fond of you, Mary.'

'And I of her. I'm afraid I shall have to disappoint her again, though.' The light was growing soft, evening scents rising from honeysuckle and jasmine. 'Theo, when John died so suddenly, I had a lot of time to think. People were kind. They tried to keep me from spending too much time alone, but I wanted solitude. I wanted to reconsider my future. I did so. I have made definite plans now.'

He saw a new light of enthusiasm come into her eyes and asked, 'Are these plans to be shared?'

'Yes, but I am only just learning to make my own plans and declare them. I suppose as a daughter and then a wife, I never had to do so before. But you will listen and not just humour me, Theo. I know you will.'

He waited. They walked the path under the trees. One

or two carriages passed, driving people home, their lanterns bobbing to the rhythm of the horses' hooves.

'John left a little money,' Mary continued. 'When he died, I had just begun helping at a school for girls. An unusual place. A high school with a full programme of subjects, but with low fees and scholarships to enable as many local girls as possible to attend. It offers them a rare chance of education. John admired the work they did. I told him about it. He would approve of my decision to go back there and join the staff.'

'You will return to India? When did you decide this, Mary?'

'Only this past week. I have enjoyed seeing Cambridge; seeing my family, seeing you, but I cannot imagine making a life here. Not any more.'

They paused, and he turned in some surprise to look at her. Lit by the gas lamps, her features were softened, her eyes sparkling. She was lovely, but with regret he registered also a distance already opening between them. Mary was removing herself. The moment made him hold her hand more tightly and press her arm into his side.

'Yes. But first I shall spend time travelling here and raising funds. I shall visit as many girls' schools and colleges as will have me. I have several appointments already. I shall find out as much as I can about girls' and women's education while I'm here. I hope to return with the most modern ideas and put them into practice there.'

'Is girls' education in high demand in Darjeeling?'

She laughed. 'It is barely even thought of! Young women in India face either endless family responsibilities or a relentless round of parties and polo and outings and tennis and dinners—with nothing to think of but what to wear and who to dance with. It suits some; it stifles others.

Many girls feel utterly confined and miserable, but without education, they have no choices. Bright girls become bitter or difficult without an outlet. So much wasted talent! I could staff ten schools with the clever women I have met who spend their days arguing over the minutiae of charity auctions and dances.'

'I am convinced! You are a fine advocate, Mary. I would donate already!'

'I imagine you did not need much convincing. I see you as a supporter of women's education. Am I right?'

'By instinct, yes, but I had not thought a great deal about that either until recently. To my shame.'

'This new acquaintance of yours has made you think about this too?'

'Yes.'

'She has had a very powerful effect, Theo, for someone you hardly know. Are you sure you are not in love?'

She was playful now. He laughed briefly, but then became more serious.

'May I ask you something about love, Mary? It would not cause you unhappiness if I mention John?'

'Not at all. I like to speak of him.'

Their path had taken them across Queen's Road and they were now strolling under the great beech trees along the Backs. A carriage passed on the road, and they listened as the sound of the horses' hooves faded slowly. One or two students in their gowns were walking merrily back from college dinners.

'How did you know that you loved John?' Theo asked. 'When first you knew him, I mean.'

She walked a little way, thinking. A water bird called somewhere on the river.

'It was not sudden, in my case,' she said, eventually. 'It

was just that everything seemed brighter, better, more promising, more interesting, more complete when I was with him. I remember saving up things to tell him. I wanted to hear every word he had to say.' She laughed and squeezed his arm. 'That is an unpoetic answer, Theo, I'm afraid, but it is the best I can do.'

They walked a little further in silence.

'I have felt such things too.'

'For the young woman you mentioned?'

'Yes. I know her only slightly, but—' he broke off.

'But what, my dear?'

'I can hardly put it into words. I feel she is of the greatest importance in my life. My future life. It is illogical, but it is a very powerful feeling.'

'That *is* love, Theo. Or at least it is the beginnings of love.'

'The other odd sensation I have,' he said, now speaking more freely, 'is that I would instantly and without hesitation give up my whole existence as it is now—abandon everything without a second thought—if it meant that I could make a life with her.'

Mary patted his arm. 'Will that be necessary?'

'It might be. '

'Is she so *utterly* unsuitable?'

'Her sister, Violet Devereaux, was involved in a fearful scandal. Have you heard of it?'

'Devereaux,' Mary repeated the name, frowning in concentration for a moment, then looked up. 'Oh yes, I know the case. We read about it in India, too. A horrible injustice, as I recall. A sickening outrage to decency.'

'Ida saw her sister's life blighted and eventually ended by it. She adopted her young nephew. They are ruthlessly persecuted to this day.'

'Poor girl. She must have needed the courage of a lioness to live through her poor sister's public disgrace. I take my hat off to her. Few of us could salvage a life worth living from such wreckage.'

'Mary, I am afraid of failing her. I have led a quiet life among books and specimens. I am not equipped for high drama. I am out of my depth. She has known tragedy, bitter struggle. My life, in comparison, has been so safe. So easy, so *low key*. My courage fails me, when I contemplate the trials that would lie ahead, if I were to… '

'To what?'

'To tell her my feelings.'

They stopped under a lamp post and Mary reached her gloved hand and put it to his cheek.

'You are braver than you think, Theo. We are all braver than we think.'

'My mother…'

Mary interrupted him, '… your mother may not be your best guide, on this occasion.'

He nodded.

A cab came their way. The horse trotting. Mary turned and raised her hand to hail the driver before turning back to him.

'Theo, losing John taught me something important: a life can change in a moment for good or ill. Some chances for happiness come once and only once. If we miss them, they are truly gone; gone forever.'

He smiled. 'Hanks says I shouldn't shilly-shally.'

The cab pulled to a stop. Theo opened the door and helped Mary inside. She leaned forward as he closed the door, and said, 'Hanks is right.'

The driver slapped the reins along the horses' backs. They began to draw away.

'What should I do?'

'Tell this young woman your feelings.'

He was walking beside the moving carriage now. 'How? She will not see me.'

'You're a clever man, Theo. You'll find a way!' Mary called.

He was left alone in the golden pool of lamplight under the trees.

Somewhere distant in the dark gardens around, a nightingale's liquid song could just be heard.

Chapter Eighteen

At luncheon, the large figure of the Master of the college sat alone at high table. He waved to Theo and pointed to the chair on his left.

'Ah, Watt, I was hoping to see you,' he said. 'You have heard, perhaps, of the situation vis-à-vis the Senior Tutorship?'

'No, Master, I have heard nothing.'

'I have accepted Rathbone's resignation. He leaves before next term. The appointments committee is seeking recommendations for his replacement.'

'I see.'

'A strong field. You are in the running. On the young side, however. Does it appeal? Senior Tutorship? Prestigious position. Great deal of responsibility.'

'Indeed.'

'You have done well, so far, Watt. Distinguished work, and so on. We have high hopes. Important to avoid any repetition of the Rathbone business, though.'

'The Rathbone business?'

'You haven't heard? Just between us, the man leaves under a cloud. Scandal over a divorcée. Frenchwoman. Newspapers got hold of it. Sensationalism, prurient gossip and so on. Frightful fuss. We wouldn't want any repetition of nonsense like that.'

Watt made no reply. A college servant served a breast of guinea fowl in aspic.

'Safe pair of hands is what we need,' the Master continued, crushing a new potato with his knife. 'Well-settled man, ideally. Married for preference, but settled and single is good enough, just as long as he is not the type to blot the college's copybook. Cause another scandal. You were considered sound in that way, as a matter of fact. Reliable. Dedicated to your research and teaching. Not likely to be caught dallying with the ladies, and so forth.' The Master gave a derisive snort. 'Your father was a fine scholar. It all helps. I believe your Mama would be your lady companion in the Senior Tutor's residence. Wise choice there. Always good to have the counsel of someone who understands the finer details of how matters work in the college.'

'You have spoken to my mother already?'

'No, no.' The Master waved such an idea aside with his fork, before adding, 'Well, I may, perhaps, have mentioned something to Mrs Watt in passing.'

Watt glared at his dish. The sound of his fellow diners at high table closed in around him. The clatter of cutlery and murmur of low conversation suddenly felt sharp and oppressive, the ancient portraits on the walls mean-eyed and cold. The Master, oblivious, was still talking about the Senior Tutorship. 'Immensely important role,' he was saying, 'powerful and respected. It is an honour even to be considered.'

At their tea time meeting, Mrs Watt was delighted. 'I told you, my dear. I told you!'

'He only mentioned it, Mama. It is a strong field, he said.'

'They always say that. I shall have a word with his wife. She will know who the other candidates are. Wisley and Parker-Jones from Peterhouse, possibly, though Wisley must be nearly seventy. You look pale, Theo. Are you coming down with something? A summer chill, perhaps? You haven't picked something up from all that swimming?'

'I am not sleeping well,' he said.

'Avoid cheese at dinner, dear. That always works. Senior Tutor! It would be a great step. No wonder you are out of sorts. The anticipation has upset your constitution.'

'You heard about Mary Tipton, Mama?'

'Yes. From her mother. She told me that Mary has taken it into her head to go back to India and teach in a school there. We are going to try to make her see sense. Her health is not up to it. Not for a moment. A widow! Alone in that country!'

'I was impressed by her dedication. She is entirely committed. I don't think you will dissuade her.'

'Is that why you are off colour, my dear? Did Mary disappoint you?'

'No. I was content to see her again, as an old friend. I would certainly not want to dissuade her from her new calling. She will succeed in pioneering the education of women and girls, I'm sure of it.'

'I do not believe in women espousing causes,' his mother remarked. 'We can't all embrace a worthy mission. Who would be left to get on with the business of marrying and raising the next generation?'

The question lingered in the air between them for a moment.

'Have you heard of the Devereaux case, Mama?' Theo asked.

'That dreadful scandal that was in the newspapers a few years ago. I have heard of it. Why do you ask?'

'I must be the only person in the country who missed it.'

'Your mind is on more important matters than the disgusting scandals of the gutter press, I hope.'

'What must it be like to be involved in such a scandal?'

'Are you thinking of Rathbone? His was a small indiscretion that took place in France. Nothing like the dreadful Devereaux case.'

'I was wondering about the family of those involved. The innocent bystanders.'

'Innocent or not, a reputation can never be salvaged. It's unshiftable, the whiff of scandal. I knew a case in my youth. I name no names, dear. The family has never recovered. They moved abroad.' His mother sighed and shuddered. 'But surely you yourself have no reason to worry on that account? Our family name has never been besmirched by anything disreputable.'

'Never?'

'Absolutely not.'

'Even in previous generations?'

'Not at all! Your father's family and my own have both been virtuous, diligent and noble-minded over many generations. You have absolutely no need to concern yourself there, Theo. You are, in fact, exactly the sort of man the college knows it can rely on as a Senior Tutor. Trustworthy, and able to give fine moral guidance to undergraduates for many years to come.'

'With your help?'

Mrs Watt lifted her chin and placed the palm of her hand over her heart. 'Any mother would be honoured to support her son in such a vital role.'

'You no longer wish me to marry, then?'

'Naturally, I still look for a happy outcome in that matter, Theo, but I no longer feel any sense of urgency. When you are Senior Tutor, I shall be able to remedy your lack of a wife by acting as your confidante myself. The Master felt this was perfectly acceptable.'

'So he *did* speak to you about this post before mentioning it to me? I thought so.'

'Oh, don't take umbrage, Theodore. It was merely a brief exchange on the way out of chapel.'

'And if I were to marry at some later time?'

His mother reached for a slice of lemon sponge. 'Well, dear, that is not likely. You have demonstrated recently that your interests lie solely in your academic work. I accept your choice.'

'And if I were to change my mind?'

Mrs Watt looked over her teacup at her son and raised an eyebrow. 'Well, dear, if the lady concerned came from a family similar to our own—one with a reputation for virtue and honesty, and with the correct social standing and intellectual prowess, then naturally I should consider it my duty to step aside and live out my old age here, *alone*.'

Hanks, who had entered the room with more hot water for the teapot, coughed quietly in the background on her way out.

'Now, Theo, I'm sorry to hurry you, but I must dress for dinner at the Downey's. The drive always takes longer than one thinks.'

On his way out, Theo carried the tea tray down to the kitchen. He found Hanks ironing a tablecloth. She cut him a piece of walnut cake to take back to college.

'What would you do, Hanks, if my mother left this house?'

Hanks, red in the face from the steam, shrugged and pressed a flatiron fiercely down onto the linen spread before her. 'Don't you worry about me, Master Theo. I keep a small boat at King's Lynn, for my own pleasure, like. I should just pack up and sail her off to sea!'

For a moment he thought she was serious, but then she let out a great chuckle and had to set the iron back on the stove for fear of dropping it. She was laughing so hard.

Chapter Nineteen

Ida always left the library by a side door. She liked the cobbled courtyard and the soft ginger of the old stonework and she liked especially the momentary view from the shady court out into the bright street through the frame of the high stone archway. As she stepped into the light this time, she saw the figure of Professor Watt leaning against the railings of Clare College opposite.

'Good afternoon, Miss Moss,' he said, stepping forward.

'Professor, this is unexpected.'

'Are you in a hurry?'

'I am expected at home.'

'Perhaps you would allow me to walk with you? I wanted to ask after the boy.'

She did not look at him, but turned along the cobbled street. 'He is well, thank you.' She spoke as if to avoid further questioning.

'Did he tell you that we knew each other?'

'He mentioned someone at the swimming lesson, but I had not made the connection. You were very kind to him.

He told me about seeing your college and he enjoys the swimming lessons with you.'

'I'm afraid that is because I am so much worse at swimming than he is. I expect he mentioned that.'

'He only said that you were always kind.'

She was hurrying, hoping to shake him off, he guessed.

'Could you spare half an hour, Miss Moss?'

'I had planned to visit the market.'

'It will be there still, in half an hour.'

'Professor Watt. You know about me now. You know about the family, our situation and so on.'

'I ask only a brief conversation,' he said. 'My college has a pleasant garden. It is nearby.'

'Why? Why did you not tell me yourself, Miss Moss?'

They were sitting on a bench beside the river shaded by an ancient weeping willow. They had already circled the gardens several times. It had taken Watt half an hour to reach the question he longed to ask. Half an hour during which their conversation had been miserably awkward and stilted. Ida's hat was on her knee. She adjusted one of three shiny cherries around the crown. Shade from the willow dappled her hair and shoulders. A mallard paddled past, its small v-shaped wake lapping gently against the riverbank.

She spoke quietly, looking away from him towards the opposite bank of the river. 'I assumed you knew. Everyone knows. The court case lasted two years. It filled the pages of every newspaper in the country. There were drawings and photographs, there were special editions, pamphlets—whole books published about it. They were music-hall songs! They sold postcards! You must have been very far buried in your studies of fish indeed if you genuinely knew nothing of the Devereaux case, professor.'

'I had vaguely heard of it, I admit.'

She looked round at him quickly, her face pale. 'Of course you had. Everybody in the country knows the case. It is years ago now and people's memories are faulty. What they forget, or never took the trouble to know, is that my sister was wholly and completely exonerated when the case finally ended. The court found in her favour. Devereaux tricked her into a feigned marriage and abandoned her without a penny when she was expecting his child. He literally threw her out onto the street. My sister begged for food on the streets of Brussels! She had nowhere to go. She slept in doorways. Nobody would take her in. Nobody believed her story. She could not reach home. She was too ashamed to write and ask for our parents' help. But somehow she endured. She found her way back to London. After a long struggle, she persuaded a lawyer to take on her case, and the court finally found in her favour and awarded damages. Of course, the wretched man never paid. Never intended to pay. He laughed in our faces as he left the court.'

She was weeping, the breath catching in her throat. Tears ran over her cheeks. Theo lost all power of reasonable thought. He could not bear to see her weep. His own throat felt tight. He leaned towards her, gripping the sides of the wooden seat. His instinct—it must be overcome—was to hold her, to take her in his arms, to comfort her.

'Miss Moss. Please. I did not intend to upset you. Please, please believe me.'

There was anger in her eyes now. 'It killed her. You know that too, I suppose.'

'No. I did not know.'

'She took her own life. I found her.' She shuddered at the memory and turned her face away.

From upriver came a small distant splash—a pike hunting, he thought.

'Oliver was less than five years old,' she added. 'I had to tell him. He could not understand. He looked for her for many months.'

This was too much for Watt. He reached a hand to her shoulder, but felt it tense and flinched away at his touch.

Ida straightened her back and dried her eyes with one of her lace gloves. She continued in a stronger voice.

'Devereaux has never ceased his persecution of us. He threatens recently to take the child. A child he denied and disowned continuously and in public throughout the court case. We are never safe.' Her voice now had a note of grim despair.

'But he has no rights over the child?'

'That means nothing to him. He is ruthless and rich. It will never end.'

She shuddered, drawing her shawl around her. 'I had allowed myself to think that we might be able to live our lives again. Here in Cambridge, there seemed to be hope of it. For years before we came here, we were hounded. Newspaper reporters came at all hours of the day and night. We were followed in the street, pointed at, hissed at. They would not serve us in shops. A doctor once refused to treat my father. People fear scandal as if it were a contagion. They forget the details. They think I am my sister.'

There was nothing he could say. He could only watch the tears run over her cheeks, his heart aching in his chest.

'We have been sent out of homes, pilloried, ridiculed, robbed. My father was attacked and beaten more than once. I have had eggs hurled at me and bricks thrown through my windows. And all by virtuous people intent on punishing sinners.'

'I'm so sorry.'

She took a deep breath. 'Well, professor, it wasn't you who threw the bricks. You were in the library all that time, studying fish—or rather, as you told me, studying the shape of the front fins of certain fossil fish.'

As she said this, she looked back at him and realised the remark had hit him harder than she intended. He had recoiled as if she had slapped him.

'My work is important to me,' he said. 'I retreat too far into it, perhaps.' They looked steadily at one another. 'I can see that it hardly seems important in comparison to the terrible events you have suffered.'

'No. No. I regret saying that. Please, I did not mean it. Forgive me.'

'I wish you would call me Theodore or Theo.'

'I was unkind, Theo. Please forgive me. It has made me a hard person, all this. And please call me Ida.'

'I do not think of you as a hard person, Ida,' he said.

Both looked across the river. The still of the late afternoon drew in around them. The bird sounds had changed. A quiet bell tolled somewhere. Small fish in shoals moved silently upstream.

His hands, clamped tightly to the bench, suddenly felt cramped. He let go, reached and took her hand in his. It was cold and clenched. He could feel her fingers cold, trembling, her glove damp. He enclosed it in both of his, to warm it.

She turned her head away.

Her glove is damp with her tears, he thought. And it is I who have made her weep. The thought was a stab.

'Ida, please...'

But she pulled her hand away suddenly. A pair of gentlemen were approaching across the lawn. They ambled genially towards the bench, deep in conversation.

'Ah, Watt,' one of them said jovially. 'Lovely afternoon. I have just been showing Doctor Lewis the planned changes to the rose garden.'

'Lewis, may I present Professor Theodore Watt, our rising star in the Natural Sciences?'

Theo stood and shook hands with the visitor.

After exchanging a few words, both gentlemen looked expectantly towards Ida, but Watt made no move to introduce her. After a moment's awkwardness, the pair nodded and moved away, sauntering back towards the college.

'You did not introduce me,' Ida said.

'I wasn't sure you would want it,' he began to explain, but Ida stood abruptly.

'Well,' she said, 'no doubt you risk your reputation by being seen in the presence of Ida Moss, sister of the notorious Violet Moss Devereaux! I shall be careful to leave by the side gate.'

'No! Ida, I did not–it was never my intention to... Ida, please!'

She waved his words aside with a gesture of her arm and walked away without turning back.

Chapter Twenty

On his afternoon walk the next day, Watt heard a bicycle behind him and Halfpenny braked and dismounted to walk alongside.

'I'm told you are openly in the running for the Senior Tutorship,' he said, slightly out of breath. 'I knew Rathbone would have to go. A French divorcée! Of course, the official reason is his post in Edinburgh, but nobody is fooled by that.'

Theo looked across the fields towards King's Chapel. 'You were hoping to make a good impression on Gwendolyn's mother, I think. Has that been successful?'

'As a matter of fact, it has. She will do her best, she said. It helped that we are both Welsh. She thinks that Gwendolyn is too young to be married, on the other hand. She is twenty-two. Neither Gwen nor I consider twenty-two is too young. Do you?'

Watt wondered how old Ida was. The question had never occurred to him. A little older, perhaps. Seventeen or eighteen at the time of the scandal. Very young.

'Watt?'

'I was just considering my answer. In general, twenty-two is not considered particularly young for marriage.'

'I impressed her with my determination to follow them to Germany if necessary.'

'Follow them? To Heidelberg?'

'Yes. I have made a decision to go there too, if they insist on taking Gwen.'

'You will leave the College? Leave your post, your teaching?'

'If necessary, yes.' They stopped, and both looked across the fields towards the colleges.

'Halfpenny! That is a very great step.'

Halfpenny shrugged. 'I can live without the College, Watt, but not without Gwen. I mean to have her. If I have to learn German and live in Germany to do so, then I shall. There is work to be had at the university there.'

'You speak German?'

'Not yet. But I have had three lessons now with a German student from St Catherine's and I think I shall find the language perfectly manageable.'

'Good heavens!' Watt said.

'That is what Gwen's mother said!' Halfpenny sounded cheerful.

'Where do you find it? This certainty? This determination?'

'I love her, Watt. I have chosen her. She has chosen me.' Halfpenny shrugged, as if all this were plain and simple.

'You never doubt it?'

'I refuse to. I want to look back as an old man and know that I did the right thing. Right from the beginning. No second chances.' Halfpenny climbed back onto his machine. 'I'm free this evening for a swimming lesson.

Oliver will not be coming. Miss Moss is keeping him at home.'

'Halfpenny, is there really nothing they can do to escape the wretched persecutions of that madman Devereaux?'

'Only move house again. For the third or fourth time.'

'It cannot be allowed to continue.'

'Who can stop him? One day, he will lose interest. Until then, they must keep moving. You will be at the pool later?'

'Is it worthwhile? I make so little progress. My chief purpose was to entertain Oliver, really.'

'Don't give up, old man. Never give up.' Halfpenny slapped him on the shoulder and pedalled away.

Instead of returning to his manuscript, Watt went to the library and requested the Deveraux papers again. The librarian brought them quickly this time, as if he had them ready.

'I found this additional item, Professor,' he said, and placed a small pamphlet on top of the folders of old newspapers. 'I thought it might be of interest.'

It was a faded pamphlet of about fifty pages, with a photograph of a baby printed on the front. It was a cheap, hurried publication—a special edition—not well reproduced. The child was in a lacy gown and bonnet. It had been propped for the photograph on a hard chair. It looked, as far as Watt could tell, confused and anxious. The caption—it made him draw breath sharply—read *The Alleged Child*. It must be Oliver.

Watt's instinct was to hurl the wretched thing across the room. The alleged child! How could even the most disgusting gutter journalist bring himself to label a child in that way? Whose choice was it to display this most innocent victim of all on the front cover?

He stood suddenly and walked to a bookshelf on the other side of the library. Its calm and orderly rows of books, each volume in its place, was reassuring. He took a deep breath.

From his desk in the distance, the librarian saw him and came over.

'Is everything in order, Professor?'

'Yes. I just find that thing difficult to read,' Watt said, indicating the pamphlet he had left on the desk.

'It is a little faded.'

'Difficult, I mean, because of the contents.'

'Ah, yes, I see,' the librarian said. 'I agree. It is tawdry and unpleasant in every way.'

'You have read it yourself?'

'Yes. I have a remote connection with the case. I thought I should inform myself. It was not an enjoyable experience.'

Watt looked at the man in surprise. He found it a challenge to imagine what connection a gentle, grey-bearded librarian in his sixties could have with a scandal like the Devereaux case. They both looked over at the pile of papers Watt had left on the table. Neither moved. Even from a distance, the cruelty they described seemed to radiate across the peaceful library.

'I also have a connection. I recently met the Moss family. Father and daughter. And the child so cruelly referred to there as the *alleged* child,' Watt said.

'Oliver,' the librarian said, quietly.

'You know the boy?'

The librarian nodded. 'We can speak in my private office, if you can spare the time.'

The librarian's room was through a discreet door and

up a coil of narrow spiral stairs, but once reached, it turned out to be comfortably spacious, with views over the river. They carried the papers up, and the librarian took the pamphlet in his hand. 'This is a repugnant and sensationalist thing, but it was printed quickly in order to raise funds to support the unfortunate lady in the case.'

'Mrs Violet Moss Devereaux?'

'She was never allowed to use his name. She remained Miss Moss throughout, officially. He denied the marriage and denied the child was his, as I expect you know. The London Gazette was the only support Violet had. They sold enough copies of this to pay her legal costs, but in order to do so, they had to appeal, I'm afraid, to human nature at its very lowest.'

'Hence the photograph of the poor child on the front cover?'

'Exactly. They set out to wring pity out of every horrible detail of the case. It worked. The British public was appalled by Deveraux and the lawyers who defended such an obvious charlatan, and they contributed generously.'

Watt shook his head. 'May I ask how you come to know the family?'

'I knew them in London. I worked in the library of the university there. It was open to members of the public. Frederick Moss, Violet's father, was a very regular visitor. He brought his girls when they were old enough. They were a scholarly trio, always picking my brains and asking me to find materials for their studies. Most unusual. I found them delightful.' The librarian smiled, remembering. 'Moss was educating himself. He loved knowledge for its own sake: Astronomy, Geology, Egyptology—it was all of interest to him. Both daughters were very enthusiastic readers. Violet won a series of scholarships. She was well on the way to a good university place when I moved here to Cambridge.'

'We lost touch then for a while. It was only much later, after all the scandal, that I met Frederick Moss here in Cambridge, in the street one day. It has all taken a huge toll on the family. He is a shadow of the man he was, but he tries to give his younger daughter and his grandson as good a life as he can. They come here to the library to read from time to time. Not quite officially, perhaps. The younger daughter is as able as her sister, but their circumstances are different now. She must work and look after the boy.'

'I have met Ida,' Watt said.

The librarian shook his head. 'One can, perhaps, imagine the child being able to escape his past—he was so young when it all happened—but it has stolen Ida's youth.'

'And Deveraux is still haunting them. He wants to seize custody of the child now.'

'I hope someone can put an end to his cruelty once and for all,' the librarian said. 'It must be possible. Perhaps you can think of something, Professor?'

Watt could only shake his head. 'Not yet,' he said. 'But, with your help, I shall continue reading everything I can about the case. There must be some clue, some key that can be found to explain his behaviour.'

'You do not accept that he is simply a monstrous bully?'

'That he undoubtedly is, but why? What does he gain by it? And more importantly, how can he be stopped?'

Chapter Twenty-One

Halfpenny found Watt sitting on the side of the pool later that afternoon, glaring fixedly into the water as if trying to burn a hole in the tiles with the power of his eyes.

'Ready, old chap?' he said.

'I did not know that such men existed,' Watt said, without looking up. 'Mine has been a sheltered life, I suppose.'

'Well… ' Halfpenny agreed, but was not sure whether it would be right to say so.

'Do you know, that *devil* Deveraux fancied himself a seaman? He liked to have his image taken in imitations of naval uniform with a sailor's side whiskers, carrying a brass telescope! The scoundrel! The utter bounder! In the photographs he is a plump little creature with the face of a turnip.'

Halfpenny could see there was nothing he could say, so he dived into the water and swam a few lengths. When he lifted his head out of the water, Watt had not moved and was still fulminating.

'Twice, Halfpenny, *twice*, he lured that poor woman into false marriage ceremonies. Have you read the case?'

'No. I hadn't the stomach for it. Gwen told me.'

'He laid siege to her for months. Followed her everywhere. Would not let her have a moment to herself, and then proposed marriage, giving her a handful of rings he had purloined from his own mother's safe without her knowledge. He swore he would die if poor Violet denied him her hand in marriage. Pretended to be sick with love. Showered her with rich gifts. Lured her onto his yacht–his pride and joy, his vastly expensive pleasure boat–and carried her off. He forced her to leave her chaperone behind and when they landed in Belgium, he drove her to a chapel where someone dressed as a priest appeared to marry them! She believed herself loved and wed in the eyes of the church. She was neither!'

'Watt, old chap. I think you should come out of the sun. You may overheat.'

'Have you ever heard anything like it? Have you, Halfpenny?'

'No. Of course not. But do come into the pool, or you will catch the sun.'

Watt slid into the pool and held onto the side. His nose was already sunburnt and his shoulders felt hot.

'I have spent the morning reading the whole story. It is hard to think of a more disreputable, lying, cruel, selfish, cowardly swine than the man who emerges from those pages. Spoilt, over-privileged, lazy, absurdly wealthy–every penny of it inherited. He is villainous and despicable in every possible way!'

'Indeed,' Halfpenny agreed, wondering whether the sunstroke had already set in. 'His family owns great swathes of Argentina with mines and rich farm lands. He can buy anything he pleases, including all the cleverest lawyers in London.'

'So I believe,' Halfpenny said.

'I mean to stop him, Halfpenny. I have skills in research. I have access to libraries. I shall study this case until I find a way!'

'Yes,' Halfpenny said, sounding doubtful. 'Now come. We will try the front crawl today. Stretch your left arm out in front.'

'I am pressed for time this afternoon,' Mrs Watt declared as she stepped into the hat shop. 'Are those *hummingbirds?* They are most becoming. Especially the green.'

'We took our inspiration from the Paris fashions,' Christabel told her, lifting a particularly fine example from its stand, ushering her customer to a chair and helping her exchange her own hat for one from the shop's new line.

'You do not think this would be too much? On a more senior lady, I mean?' Mrs Watt looked at herself in the mirror, turning her head left and looking back at her reflection out of the corner of her eye. 'It is for a formal college occasion.'

'Not at all.'

Mrs Watt considered. 'I should not want to attract too much attention to myself.'

'The perfect hat *never* attracts too much attention,' Christabel said. 'It simply completes its wearer by adding an elegantly understated finishing touch.'

Mrs Watt turned her head the other way so that she could glimpse the tiny bird on that side of the brim.

'I must admit, it is rather splendid. If I had my way, the feathers would extend just a little further. Along the brim and out to the back, I think.'

'That can be done. As a matter of fact, the maker of the hummingbirds is here in the shop this afternoon. Ida, Mrs Watt here would like to discuss a slight alteration.'

Ida came forward from the corner.

'Could the tail feathers be longer?' Mrs Watt removed the hat and held it towards Ida. 'So that they were a touch more prominent?'

'Of course. Would that be in green?'

'Green and black, perhaps? And about so long?'

'Curling beyond the brim? Certainly.'

'You are most obliging.'

'Would a week be soon enough?' Christabel asked.

'A week would be most acceptable. I shall collect it myself. Now, I was hoping for a word with your sister.'

'Lucia is not here. Perhaps I can pass a message to her?'

'You could tell her that her services will no longer be needed.'

'I see. She will be sorry to hear that.'

'I shall pay her fee, as agreed. But the service she provided is no longer necessary.'

'I hope you were not displeased with my sister's efforts.'

'Not at all. It is a most satisfactory outcome. My son's plans have altered. He is to take on a very important role in his college–in the university as a whole. He will not marry now. He will have no time. He will dedicate himself entirely to college life, and his work.'

The bell on the door rang out as Mrs Watt left the cool shade of the shop and hurried out into the bright street.

'That is the professor of fish's mother,' Christabel

remarked as they watched her stride away. 'You saw him that time, I think.'

'I did,' said Ida. She looked at the little bird on the hat in her hand. Its head was made from the wooden acorn they had both found at the market.

Chapter Twenty-Two

In the Porter's Lodge, Bill Parker was patiently explaining mealtimes to a puzzled visiting scholar. Watt waited in the background, checking his pigeonhole unnecessarily for post. When Parker was alone, Watt approached.

'What can I do for you, Professor?' Bill asked.

Watt hesitated, but then seemed to make himself press on. 'You were a military man once, Bill, I believe?'

'Yes, Sir. The Blues and Royals, but that would be a few years ago now.'

'They taught you to fight, I imagine. In the army?'

'Yes, Sir. Battlefield tactics, hand-to-hand combat, and so on.' Bill held his fists up in the manner of a boxer, and punched the air a couple of times.

'Good,' Watt said, 'excellent!' He shifted from one foot to the other. 'And you remember? You remember how to do it?'

'To do what, Sir?'

'To fight. You remember how to fight a man?'

'It isn't something you forget, Sir. And I have been called upon to do so once or twice since, even here at the Porter's Lodge.'

'Ah, you have? Very good,' Watt said. 'I should like you to teach me, if you could possibly spare the time.'

'Teach you?'

'Teach me how to do it. How to go about fighting someone? How does one start, for example?'

'You could have knocked me down with a feather!' Bill said later over a pint in the Baron of Beef.

'Is he a strong bloke? Can he handle himself? What did you tell him?' asked his drinking companion, a Head Gardner.

Bill laughed into his beer. 'Strong? No. Nothing to him. What put the idea into his head, I'll never know. He meant it, though.'

'What d'you tell him?'

'Go in fast, I said. Go for him before he goes for you and aim central. The nose, because that hurts, or the solar plexus to knock the wind out. One good hard blow.'

His companion nodded. 'Then what?'

Bill took a swig, gulped it down, and smiled. 'Then run for your bloody life!'

In the pool, later, Halfpenny floated on his back like a starfish looking up at the sky. Watt, whose attempts to float on his back had not been so successful, held the side and kicked his legs.

'Halfpenny, do you mind if I ask whether you have ever been in a fight?'

'A few,' Halfpenny replied without moving. 'At school.'

'What does it entail?'

'Somebody hits you and you hit them back, or the other way around,' Halfpenny said drowsily.

'Have you ever started a fight?'

'Not since I was nine. A nasty piece of work called Riverton broke my catapult.'

'How did you go about that?'

'I gave him a shove.'

'On the shoulder?'

'Probably the shoulder. Why are you asking this?'

'I intend to fight Devereaux.'

The shock made the sleepy starfish jerk and almost sink. 'You must be mad! He'll kill you.'

'I have a theory about him. I re-read the papers about the case and Violet Moss's own account. I have discovered two important things about him.'

'Did you discover that he cannot raise his arms above waist height? Something of that sort would be useful if you intend to engage him in fisticuffs.'

'No. He is perfectly fit and able, unfortunately for me. But as I read the papers, it came to me that he is a pampered coward, Halfpenny. He picks on women and children to bully. Or animals. There is an account of him throwing kittens into a well for sport. When he twisted an ankle walking in the Alps, he wept and moaned for so long that everyone assumed he was mortally injured. He hates and fears pain of any sort. I believe that if I beat him thoroughly, he will leave them alone. Nobody has done it so far. They have used the courts. They have tried to use reason against him. Reason will never work. He is a monomaniac. An obsessive. A physical beating might be enough of a shock to stop him.'

'Watt, even if that were true, you *yourself* may not be the man to do it. Your powers are intellectual, rather than physical. Have you ever given anyone a beating?'

'A beating? I have hardly even been impolite to anyone so far. But watch me, Halfpenny, I shall now breaststroke from here to the other side of the pool, as a mark of my determination.'

And he did. More or less.

'You are very red, Theo, my dear. I hope it is not a chill on the kidneys from the swimming. At your age, it is not wise to take such risks.'

Mother and son were in the garden where the tea was being served by the pond under the shade of the great walnut tree. Pale lilies flowered out of the green depths and damsel flies skipped over the water's surface.

Hanks handed Theo a cup of tea and a generous slice of her best cherry cake.

'Risks,' Theo said. 'As a matter of fact, I should like to discuss risks.'

'By the way, the Master's wife says they leave for Yorkshire early next week, so if he wants to dine with you, it will have to be soon. Thursday would be my guess.'

'I have never taken any risks, have I?'

His mother was not listening. 'The servants in the Senior Tutor's house are very well-regarded. The butler has been there for nearly thirty years. There is only a plain cook for everyday, but you can have a chef from the College kitchens for entertaining. A fair amount of entertaining is expected, as you can imagine. I can help with that, of course. In fact, Theo, I wonder whether it might not be best if I were to join you at the Senior tutor's residence? It is a large establishment for a single man to manage. What do you think, dear?'

'I think we should not count our chickens.'

'That is a very common expression. I'm surprised at you.' Mrs Professor Watt looked pained and sipped her tea. A large frog pushed his head out of the water at the edge of the pond and watched them.

'The rest of what I have to say may shortly surprise you still further, mother, I'm afraid,' Watt said. 'I have met a young woman…'

His mother's hand jerked, causing her teacup to rattle in its saucer. She blinked at him, eyes wide.

'This may take some time to explain,' he said. 'You may know her. She works occasionally in a hat shop you visit. Her name is Ida Moss.'

'She is a shop assistant?'

'Occasionally. She also works in the University Library.'

'And you mention this Moss person because…?'

'Because I care for her, Mama. It has taken a great deal of time to recognise it, but I find I do care for her. I wish to… that is to say, I intend to… '

'And her family?' his mother interrupted.

'Well, there lies the potential problem. Her sister was involved in a great scandal. Ida, herself…'

'Not the Deveraux case!'

'How did you know?'

'You mentioned the wretched scandal recently. It stuck in my mind.'

'It was Ida's sister, Violet, who was at the centre of it. The courts found in her favour, but the public humiliation was too much. It led to her death. It robbed her son of his mother.'

'Oh, good heavens.' Mrs Watt loosened the lace collar at her neck and fanned herself with her hand. 'Oh my word! I dread to think what the Master would make of such a thing.'

'The Master?'

'The Master of the college. He would be appalled to hear you were associating with… '

'With what? What is the end of that sentence?'

'With someone so steeped in scandal. Scandal is what he most fears. It would bring the college into the worst kind of disrepute.'

'Why? Ida is perfectly innocent! She is a victim!'

'That may be, but the taint of the Deveraux affair is all about her. She will never shake it off. Never! How could she? I find it difficult to imagine a more utterly unsuitable young woman from the college's point of view, and my own.'

The sun slid behind a cloud. Theo could see mosquito larvae wriggling in the pond as the shadow passed over.

'Do you realise what you are saying, Mama? You are condemning an innocent young woman.'

'It is not I who condemns her. It is decent society as a whole! I am merely realistic. She will never shake off the damage to her family's reputation. I am sorry for that, but we must be practical. Why should I stand by and allow my own family's reputation, and your career, to be polluted by association with hers?'

'Is that what you believe? Truly? That any connection with Miss Moss or her family would damage us?'

His mother hesitated. She lifted her chin. 'Why take the chance? You are on the brink of a step in your career that will be the making of you. Of *us*! You cannot, surely, be considering throwing all that away on some chit of a girl whose sister's reputation has been mauled and shredded by every scandal sheet in the country!'

'That is exactly what I am considering. She is a true-hearted innocent who has been forced to endure year after year of public vilification. Despite all of this, she has managed to make a happy enough household to raise a kind and lovable young nephew.'

'How well are you acquainted with this hat seller, Theo? You can hardly know her! No doubt she has a pretty face, but you would tire of her company within a fortnight. I blame myself. I have allowed you to bury yourself in academic work to the detriment of other aspects of your life. You are an innocent. Many learned gentlemen are. They know nothing of the world. They are easily lured into relationships by the more worldly sort of woman. I have seen it before, many times. I had thought better of you, Theo, frankly. I did not expect such impulsively juvenile behaviour from you. This is why the guiding hand of a mother is so essential.'

'I am sorry, Mother, that this same guiding hand so ruthlessly swats aside my own feelings. It condemns Miss Moss to shame and persecution and her nephew to fear and poverty. Have you no doubts about the propriety of this, mother? Are you absolutely certain that you are in the right?'

'Theo!'

Mrs Watt gasped and pressed a hand to her bosom, but her son did not stay to see the gesture.

Half an hour later, when Hanks went to offer sherry, she was surprised to find her employer sitting in the darkening garden staring at the pond alone. It was unusual for Master Theo to leave without a visit to the kitchen. It was unusual for his mother to sit silently in the shadows. The cake was untouched.

Hanks didn't like the look of things at all.

Chapter Twenty-Three

Too restless, after leaving his mother's house, to go back to his own rooms, Watt found himself in the library. The librarian had set the papers about the Devereaux case aside in a quiet corner, and Watt settled there to read further. Every detail confirmed him in his low opinion of Devereaux, but, more detached now, he made notes and found he was left with questions that were not easily answered.

Why, he wondered, had Devereaux suddenly decided that he wanted the child? He had spurned and repudiated him—his complete denial of any connection with Oliver featured in newspaper headlines throughout the trail—but now, years later, he had suddenly decided the same child was indeed his and must be seized. It made no sense.

'Why?' he asked, without realising he said it aloud.

The librarian approached, concerned. 'Is all well, Professor Watt?'

'Have you read the details of the case yourself, Chapman?'

'Yes. I have. I, like you, was searching for something—anything—that might help Mr Moss and his family.'

'And did you find anything? I have concluded, for example, that Deveraux is a coward, physically. He may be full of bluster and bullying, but there is good evidence that he is terrified of physical conflict.'

The librarian brought a chair and sat at the desk beside Watt. He nodded. 'I agree. But short of hiring a gang of thugs to pounce on him, I can't see how that would help.'

'I might confront him myself!' Watt declared.

Chapman said nothing, but shook his head. 'I had to admit defeat in the end. I could find nothing in these papers that offered an obvious way of shaking him off. Endless funds give Deveraux tremendous power.'

'But are they endless? I keep asking myself why Deveraux suddenly wants the child now,' Watt said.

'It is a puzzle, certainly. Can you advance any theories?'

'I increasingly believe it is something to do with his mother.'

'His mother? Mrs Deveraux? She seems to have played little part in all this,' Chapman looked over the pile of documents spread across the table.

'She is rarely mentioned in the newspaper reports because she distanced herself so thoroughly from the whole court proceedings, but I believe she is still the power that controls Deveraux. Perhaps the only power he accepts,' Watt told him.

'She is elderly, surely?'

'She is, if she is still living at all.'

'And you think she might have done or said something that persuaded her son to try taking the child?' Chapman sounded unconvinced.

'As I said, I have read these papers thoroughly, and I can think of no other explanation. It is almost certainly something to do with money. He lives an extremely extravagant life. No expense is spared, with his yachts and his grand parties. It is only speculation, but I wonder whether Devereaux has acquired debts large enough to trouble even him. He has perhaps convinced himself that if he presents himself to his mother as a responsible father, she might be more generous.'

'His mother still holds the purse-strings?'

'She does. Although the family is extremely wealthy, it is Mrs Deveraux who inherited, and she who remains in control of the whole fortune. Deveraux himself has no direct access to it. He depends on an allowance. His mother pays that allowance. He is entirely in her power. He attempted to rid himself of Violet Moss when she announced that she was expecting his child. The speculation was that he had not told his mother about the so-called marriage, and was terrified that Mrs Deveraux would cut him off without a penny. She has the power to do so.'

'But she continued to support him throughout the case. And since,' said Chapman.

'He still lives the same profligate life so far, but perhaps something has changed. I wonder if his mother might be growing tired of his ways.'

Watt and the librarian both looked again at the piles of old newspapers spread on the desk before them.

'Can we discover where Mrs Deveraux lives?' Watt asked.

'We hold all the street directories,' Chapman said. 'It should not be too difficult to find her.'

'Good. Then perhaps I should pay her a visit.'

Over dinner, Will Halfpenny remarked that Watt looked distracted. 'You are miles away, Watt.'

'Apologies. I am preoccupied tonight. Preoccupied with mothers, as it happens.'

'Mothers are of great interest to me too,' Will said. 'Specifically, how to persuade them.'

'You are still attempting to convince Gwendolyn's mother that you are a suitable match?'

'I have had some success. She has agreed to put my case to her husband. She and Gwendolyn have hatched a plan to take him punting and work their magic on him with a picnic.'

Watt couldn't help smiling. There really was something magical about a summer picnic on the river.

'And is it your own mother who needs persuasion?' Will asked.

They were eating a delicate salmon mousse, presented in the form of a fish, with cucumber scales and caviar eyes.

'I broached the idea of my forming a connection with Ida Moss.'

'You did?' Halfpenny looked up sharply. 'And how did your mother react?'

'She believes it would end my career and blight my academic life forever.'

They both ate a little more of the mousse.

'She may be right,' Will said eventually.

'Yes. But she may not. Besides, I have come to the unilateral decision that I should declare my feelings to Ida, and take immediate steps to rid her and her family permanently of the dreadful Deveraux.'

'By punching him on the nose?'

'If necessary, yes. But by speaking to his mother first.'

'Heavens!' Will Halfpenny said. 'Where did that idea come from?'

'From the library. Where all the best ideas are found,' Watt told him, as the asparagus tart arrived.

The boy was in bed. His aunt, sitting by his feet, leaned over to show him the illustrations in the book she had been reading aloud.

'Aunt Ida, will you be married one day?' the boy asked suddenly.

She blinked at him. The question had come from nowhere. 'Why do you ask, Oliver?'

'I only wondered. I asked grandfather, but he didn't know. I think you should be married. You could have your own house. Grandfather and I will look after each other very well. Or perhaps you could have the house next door and bring us our dinner sometimes.'

'And who would want to marry me?' said his aunt, closing the book and smiling at the boy.

'A kind gentleman.'

'Do you know any?'

The boy considered this question for a moment before replying. 'I know two. One is Doctor Halfpenny, but he loves Miss Hurst.'

'How do you know that?'

'His face goes all pink when he sees her. And he always wants to talk about her. If I want to distract him from the swimming lesson, I just say something about Miss Hurst. He forgets everything else straight away. It works the other way round, too.'

Ida laughed. 'And who is the other kind man you know?'

'He has swimming lessons with me. His name is Professor Watt, but I am allowed to call him Theo. He once came here with your parasol. That was kind. He rescues ladybirds and beetles if they fall in the swimming pool. That is kind too. He likes fish best. We talk about fish or mathematics sometimes while Dr Halfpenny is demonstrating one of his swimming strokes. Theo thinks Dr Halfpenny might be half dolphin because he swims so well.'

The boy had pulled up the covers, and was beginning to drowse.

Ida was no longer smiling. 'It's time you went to sleep, my dear.'

'They bring you very good cake if you go to Theo's college,' the boy said, closing his eyes.

'Cake, even good cake, is not a good enough reason to marry someone,' said Ida, kissing his cheek sadly before she left.

'And besides,' she added to herself on the way downstairs, 'Professor Watt is destined for high office, and his reputation must not be blotted by the likes of us.'

Professor Solomon came over to Ida's table in the library. He smiled, watching as she used tweezers to tease tiny fragments of parchment apart. A row of fragments were drying on the blotting paper in front of her.

'Do you know what these fragments are?'

Ida paused and shook her head. 'No. They have scraps of writing on them, but not in any language I know.'

'In this culture,' Solomon said, 'there was a tradition of writing a few final words before death. A death-bed message to those who remained.' He pulled a stool over and began examining the fragments Ida had separated. 'Many of the pieces we find are fragments of such notes. They tend to be short–a sentence or two only–they were intended to comfort those who remained, and to offer them a little wisdom.'

He pointed to one of the fragments with a pencil he drew from his pocket.

'Here you see is part of a word we find very often. In fact, it is the most common word in these fragments. It means love.'

Ida peered at the faint curl of writing on the tiny piece of parchment.

'Sometimes the death bed messages say something about money or land or property, but this word is by far the most common.'

'What do they say about love?' Ida asked him.

'They almost always warn the reader not to miss it,' Solomon said with a smile. '*Listen to your heart; do not miss the call of love; take a chance when love comes; follow the inclinations of your heart*; that sort of thing is very common. I find it touching. Very little changes in human life, it seems.'

He stood. 'Your work is exemplary, Ida.'

'I enjoy it immensely,' she said.

'Good.' Solomon straightened up and put his reading glasses back into his pocket. 'But don't forget to live your own life.'

The professor's letter, unopened, was in her pocket. It had been delivered that morning. As Dr Solomon left the room, she decided it was time to open it. She found it hard to explain to herself why she had delayed so long. She didn't know what she hoped for. Or what she dreaded. Or if she hoped for and dreaded the same thing. She walked over to one of the tall windows and used a blade they kept for cutting parchment to slit the envelope. Standing in the shaft of summer light that cut a bright angle through the dim interior of the conservation room, she pulled out the letter and began to read.

Dear Ida,

I once studied a strange fish called the olm. It is a pale, blind, worm-like animal found only in deep caves, the kind of creature only naturalists find appealing. The olm is a curiosity. It lives to a great age—people have kept them for eighty years—and has tiny legs and arms with hands like a lizard's. It breathes using fronded external gills.

Forgive this excursion into the life of remote caves. I have a purpose.

I worked on the olm and kept a dark tank of them. I recorded their habits. I became fond of my olms. Their solitary life browsing microscopic organisms in the mud appeared so innocent, harmless, peaceful, and content. It seemed to me that it represented some sort of natural ideal. But one day in one of my experiments, I shone a light into their dark tank. To my great surprise, a few of the little creatures slowly left their muddy homes and paddled to the surface, something I had never observed before. Olms have no eyes, so some organ or instinct as yet unknown must have reacted to the rays of light. Rising to the surface in nature would expose them to predators. They are utterly defenceless. Their food is in the mud, so what made them quit their sanctuary and swim upwards?

At first there was speculation among my colleagues that these excursions were mating opportunities—the May Balls of the olm world. This I disproved. I demonstrated that most olms meet and pair in the mud. They do not need to make a long, difficult journey. They can ignore a brief sunbeam piercing the quiet dim of their world. Only a few take the chance and swim up. Nobody knows why.

I apologise if I am exhausting your patience. I have no other way to express the change I have felt since I covered myself in mud and you rescued a rather handsome chub in the stream that day. I have never met anyone like you.

I make no assumptions, Ida. I have no idea why my instincts tell me that it is vitally important to direct my life towards you in just the way my olms directed themselves towards the light. I have no explanation. All I know is that those are my feelings.

I do not pretend to understand what your life has been like for the last few years. I cannot imagine being menaced and persecuted, much less publicly savaged and vilified. I have never had to flee my home or live secretly. I do not have to look over my shoulder or constantly expect the return of a vicious enemy. I have not lost a beloved sibling or taken in a motherless child.

At first, I thought that heartfelt sympathy was all I could offer. I feel differently now. I want to rid you of your persecutor once and for all. This is not contingent on our friendship developing further, nor do I hope for gratitude. My motivation is to correct a terrible injustice.

If I appeared to avoid introducing you to my colleagues the other day, Ida, it was not because I feared their judgement. Another thing I have realised in the past few days is how little such opinions matter to me. I hesitated because I did not know whether you yourself would want your name exposed to them. Naturally enough, you came to another conclusion. I was wrong. I hurt your feelings. I apologise.

I salute the courage it has taken you to find a little equilibrium and peace amongst all this. You must have found some. How else could Oliver be such a fine boy? He is a credit to you and your father. With no advantages except your strength, loyalty and love, he is developing into a good-hearted and thoughtful boy with a curiosity that suggests quick intelligence. You should both be very proud of him.

You may write to me at my College, if you should wish. I will understand perfectly if you do not. I love you, Ida. There, that is me, defenceless as an olm, swimming towards the light, towards you.

Sincerely yours,
Theo Watt

PS Unlike an olm, I am, in reality, a very poor swimmer, Oliver will probably have mentioned that.
TW

Chapter Twenty-Four

'I hope Ida brings the next hummingbirds soon. I have at least three customers waiting for a hat with one. I'm running short of cherries as well.'

Christabel straightened a row of five straw boaters on their stands in the shop window, then stepped back to inspect them, frowned and unstraightened them again so that each was at a different jaunty angle.

'She is a shy creature,' Lucia said from her stool in the corner. 'We know nothing of her, really, except that she now works in the university library, of all places.'

'Her handiwork is excellent. She is reliable when she works here. I have left her in charge once or twice. I do not trust everyone to take care of the shop, as you know.'

'She has a sad air lately.'

'That is not good for sales,' Christabel said. 'Ladies like a bright spirit of cheerfulness about them when they purchase a hat.'

'Nobody can be brightly cheerful every day of the year.'

'Perhaps not, but one must assume the air of bright cheerfulness in the shop, if necessary.'

Lucia put on a ghastly grin of mock cheerfulness to irritate her sister. 'I have the strangest new client,' she said, when the grin faded. 'A man called Dixon. He wants me to follow his fiancé to see where she goes on a Thursday afternoon. She says she goes to a ladies' meeting, but he is not convinced she has told him the truth.'

'He sounds a cad to me,' Christabel remarked. 'What she does on a Thursday is her own concern, surely.'

'Well, you and I might think so, but Mr Dixon wants to know what his beloved is up to.'

'Did you accept his commission?'

'I said I would consider the matter and let him know. He did not flinch at a fee of three guineas.'

Christabel looked impressed. 'It's Thursday today.'

'Yes. I think I'll follow her this afternoon and see where she goes. It shouldn't be difficult. I know her address.'

'And then report back to the over-curious Mr Dixon?'

'Well, perhaps. It depends what I find out.'

The Moss family's door was closed, but to his surprise, it was thrown open at his first knock. A broken window pane had been temporarily repaired with brown paper.

Mr Moss stood squarely in the doorway wearing a striped apron. 'No umbrella this time?' he demanded.

'It was a parasol,' Watt told him, but then regretted the correction as Mr Moss glared and stepped back as if the close the door. Watt could see packing cases in the house behind him. 'Mr Moss, I should be greatly obliged if you would permit me a short interview.'

Moss looked him witheringly up and down. 'I'm busy, as you can see,' he said. 'What could you want with me, anyway?'

'May I step inside?'

'We don't allow visitors. We've had all the trouble we need.' He closed the door. The familiar brass knocker was level with Watt's nose.

'Mr Moss, I do understand…'

'You do not understand!' Moss called from behind the door. 'If you understood, you would go away and leave us alone! Everybody else would too! Just clear off.'

Watt could now hear banging and clattering sounds, as if hard objects were being thrown into wooden tea chests. He looked up and down the street. Several people were already standing on their doorsteps, looking his way. Even at a distance, they were clearly taking their neighbour's side. It was a pleasantly warm afternoon. Two small boys with bare feet and ill-assorted clothes sat themselves on the opposite pavement to get a good view.

'I want only to offer you some help, Mr Moss,' Watt said, trying to pitch his voice loudly enough to be heard, but quietly enough to share as little of this information as possible with the listeners, who leaned their ears his way.

'Leave off and go away!' Moss replied, but Watt thought he detected a shift in his tone. After a pause, he added, 'What sort of help could someone like you be to us?'

'I will explain if you let me in, Sir.'

The door opened. Moss stood aside and let Watt in. 'You must not be here when they come home. My daughter and my grandson. They are anxious,' he said, 'and with good reason.' He gestured towards the window.

'You seem to be packing,' Watt said. The floor was half taken up with tea chests.

'The landlord has given us notice to quit.' He said this with a shrug. 'It's something quite usual for us. No surprise.'

'Have you somewhere to go?'

'Not yet. We had hoped that this would be a permanent… ' Moss's truculence suddenly failed him. He bent over with his hands on his knees and took several deep breaths. 'I am feeling my age, Professor. I am not as young as I was once.'

'You know who I am, then?'

'I remember, and Ida has mentioned you. I would not have let you in unless she had said you were decent to her— and to the boy.'

'She has told me your family's story.'

'We don't hide it. We can't.' Moss sat suddenly on a stool and wiped his brow with a handkerchief. 'They are dearer to me than life itself, Watt. But I am worn down. I can't keep the brute away.'

'If I can help you, I should like to do so.'

'What can you do? Everything has failed.'

'I believe he can be stopped.'

'Powerful men have tried. He defies the law of the land and all its officers. If you only knew what he has done to my family.' Moss shook his head. His face was weary.

'I am not deterred.'

'He will find us again.'

'No, that is going to end.'

'It is not going to end! Better men that you have failed to end it for years!'

'I know that, but they did not feel towards your daughter as I do. I have taken the liberty of sending her a declaration of my intentions.'

Moss was brought up short by this. He glared at Watt

through narrowed eyes. 'She will go nowhere without the boy.'

'I would never ask it of her. My plans include the boy and yourself.'

Moss pulled at the scarf he had round his neck. He looked out of the back window for a long minute. When he turned back to Watt, his bearing had altered. 'How do I know you are sincere and not exploiting an unfortunate young woman? Taking advantage of our misfortune in some disgraceful way?'

'You have only my word for that.'

Moss made a cynical face. 'How can you support her, if I were to consider it? What are your earnings?'

Watt told him what the allowance from Trinity College had been the previous year. It was a substantial amount. Moss blinked and looked back in frank astonishment. 'You should be warned, though, that I may not be able to continue at Trinity. Leaving would reduce that very considerably.'

'Why would you leave?'

'I would leave if the college made it difficult for me to continue.'

'Difficult because of us? Because of Ida and the whole story?'

'Yes.'

'You would leave and choose Ida?'

'I would, Sir.'

'I have no reason to trust what you say.'

'I accept that. It is only to be expected.'

Moss glanced at him again, then abruptly held out his hand. Watt shook it. 'Are you a practical man?' the older man asked. 'Can you make things? Repair them? Cook? Drive a carriage? Grow vegetables?'

'I can do none of those things.'

'Well, God help us all, in that case,' Moss said, but he said it with a smile.

Chapter Twenty-Five

The Deveraux residence was as secretive as a large house in a city street can be. Its boundary walls were so tall, its hedges and garden borders so overgrown, that the gate and driveway up to the front door were almost hidden from view. To a passer-by, the house looked dark, shuttered, empty, forbidding. *Go away*, it told the world. To Theo Watt on a bright summer's morning, it presented a series of challenges. The first of these was how to reach the front door. The second was how to persuade suspicious staff to allow him to speak to the owner. If she was there at all.

He stood and looked at the house through the undergrowth and wondered how he came to be there. It was complicated. But then he thought of Ida that day in the stream with her hat blown off and her dress floating in muddy water, and he thought of Oliver offering him a toffee and in he went through the bramble-tangled front gate, forcing his way through until he felt gravel under his feet and emerged onto what remained of a driveway.

It was soon clear that a gardener was still employed in

this part of the garden. Close to the house, beds of flowers, roses in particular, still thrived. They were well cared for. This seemed hopeful to Theo, eager for good omens. As he rounded a corner and saw the porticoed front door ahead, he also spotted a hunched figure in a large veiled hat and leather gauntlets working in a rose bed. She did not see him, but continued dead-heading, collecting the spent rose blossoms in a wicker basket.

Not wanting to startle this lady, he cleared his throat and shuffled his feet on the gravel to warn her of his approach. She heard and froze with her fingers on the stem of a withered rose.

'Good morning. I am Professor Theodore Watt from Cambridge,' he said.

The lady's only response was to bow her head and turn away. She reminded him of a startled hedgehog curling itself up.

'I am hoping to speak to Mrs Antoinette Deveraux.'

The lady slowly raised her head to look at him. She scrutinised his appearance for several long minutes, then said, 'What has he done now?'

This reply took Theo so much by surprise that he took a moment to gather his thoughts. But such a bald question called for a similar reply, so he said, 'He is threatening to remove his estranged son by force. To kidnap him. The boy is only ten. He has suffered a great deal…'

'And what do you imagine I can do about it, Professor?' the old lady demanded, returning to her rose bush. 'My son is a grown man. He does not consult me on his actions. Far from it!'

She turned back to her rose bush, cutting the stem she was holding and adding the dead rose to her basket. She was an elegant lady beneath her gardening overalls, he noted. Lace and several strings of pearls showed at her neck.

'You still hold some influence over your son, I believe,' Watt said.

'That is none of your business. You are intruding. Please leave my garden before I call for assistance.'

'I mean you no harm, Madam, but I must urge you to use any powers you have over your son to keep him away from the boy. It will end in catastrophe.'

The old lady slowly bent and set her wicker basket and secateurs on the path. She then straightened herself to her full height and looked piercingly at Theo from under the brim of her hat.

'His life is ruined. My life is ruined. What further catastrophes are you imagining?'

'If he takes the boy by force, he will be caught and jailed for kidnap.'

'The courts are powerless where my son is concerned. He does as he pleases. He always has.'

'Those were *civil* courts, Madame. If he kidnaps Oliver, your son will be tried and jailed in the criminal courts.'

The old lady looked away towards the house. 'My servants will remove you by force, if I call,' she said, but then paused and added, 'Oliver? You say the boy's name is Oliver?'

'It is. He is ten years old. He likes mathematics. He is learning to swim.'

'Oliver,' the old lady repeated. 'I did not know that.' She looked towards the house.

Theo was puzzled at first, but then realised that in all the records he had read of the case, the child's name had never been mentioned. He was called 'the child', or 'the infant' or even 'the alleged child'. Oliver's name had never been made public, not even to his grandmother.

Mrs Deveraux removed her gardening gloves and threw back the veil on her hat. White hair framed her strongly featured face. She turned bright, dark eyes to Theo and assessed him with a cold look from head to toe. 'I have not spoken to my son since the court case began. We have no contact. I do not read newspapers. I am aware of the basic facts of the matter, but I have excluded as much as possible of the sordid and repellent story from my existence. Who could blame me for that? The cost to me has been high. I live here in isolation. My name is known and forever connected with the case. I thought of moving away. Another country. Another continent, even. But this is my home. These are my roses. What is there for me anywhere else?'

A tall uniformed manservant, a strongly built young man, hurried down the front steps of the house and approached them. The old lady help a hand up to stop him. 'Allard, I shall take tea with this visitor in the orangery.'

'Tea, Madam?' he seemed startled.

'In the orangery, as I said.'

The servant looked hard at Theo, then turned on his heel and retraced his steps.

'You will join me for tea. Guests are rare here, but we have not entirely forgotten our manners, I hope.'

Thinking back to this strange encounter later, Theo remembered being led through the dim interior of the house to a large, warm conservatory filled with palms and rows of citrus trees in huge terracotta pots.

'I imagine you are a professor of law,' Mrs Deveraux

had said. 'My callers tend to be lawyers. Or scandal mongering journalists, but we haven't seen one of those for a while, have we, Allard?'

'No, Madam,' the butler had agreed. He had set a tea tray under a tree covered in lemons. The scent of them was all around.

'Natural History is my subject, as it happens,' Theo told her.

'Animals?' she asked, 'Plants? Rocks?'

'Fish.'

'Fish! My word!' she said. 'A professor of fish. Imagine that!'

It was not the first time someone had reacted with patronising incredulity to his life's work. Theo made no reply.

'Tell me your motive for coming here, Professor...' she had forgotten his name.

'... Watt,' he reminded her.

'... it is a long enough journey from Cambridge, after all. What possible interest could a professor of fish have in my family?'

She handed him a cup of tea. He was not invited to add sugar or milk. Tea was served as the hostess decreed in this house.

'I am a friend of your grandson's family. That is all. The boy lives with his grandfather and his aunt. They are good people.'

'You think that if I become interested in my grandson, I will exert some influence over my son? Is that right? That is your motive for telling me about him?'

'My only hope is to prevent more misery from being dealt to a boy who has already had the most difficult start in life. He is a happy child, despite it all. But he lives—they all live—in constant fear of your son. Deveraux haunts the very streets where they live. Oliver has been brought up to hide and be wary at all times. This is not the way a child should have to live. His aunt and grandfather have moved house countless times because of this persecution. If your son does not menace them himself, he writes anonymous letters and spreads rumours that lead to their vilification by others.'

The old lady settled the pearls at her neck and looked away, taking his words in as she stirred the teapot.

'I was not aware of the extent of this behaviour,' she said after a while. She sounded reluctant to admit as much, and pressed her lips together, as if to prevent herself from saying more.

A long silence fell, during which Theo listened to the bees buzzing in the citrus blossom and the song of a London blackbird somewhere outside.

'If you hold any power over your son, I beg you to use it to free this family from persecution.'

'He has never listened to me. Not since he was a boy. Motherhood has brought me only misery since his late father sent Edward to school. Everything changed then. He was a pleasant child until that time. Something changed. He lost moral judgement. I cannot explain it. But he remains my son. My only child.'

'It has not been easy. I can see that.' Theo said.

'You can have no idea, professor. Few can imagine how my life has been through all this.'

'No. But you have a chance to end some of the suffering your son is causing. You still control the finances that govern him.'

'I said before that is none of your business, Sir.'

'A single letter. A clause added to a settlement. A sentence restricting his movements—preventing him from living in this country, for example—would be enough to give Oliver the chance of an ordinary life. You could write a letter this afternoon that would give your grandson the freedom to look optimistically into his own future for the very first time.'

She looked sharply at him. 'And why should I alienate my only son to benefit this disputed child I know nothing of?'

'Because Oliver is your grandson. Because he is a lovable, innocent child who deserves a chance.'

'You say so, but I have no evidence that this Oliver even exists, much less that he is my grandson. There have been so many lies over the years. There have been times when straightforward truth has been eliminated from my whole existence. I could hold fast to nothing but my garden and my plants. No human being could be trusted.'

'It has been dreadful. I don't doubt it.' Theo said. 'You need time. Here is my card. You have only to write to me.'

She took it with a sceptical look.

'And what, Professor, is your *real* interest in Oliver and his family?'

Theo set his cup and saucer on the edge of the table. 'As I said, I am a friend of the family.'

'Is that all?' They looked each other in the eye for a moment. Theo felt the pulse beat in his own neck as he met the older lady's flinty gaze.

'I hope to marry Oliver's aunt,' he said, finally.

'Ah! Now we have it,' she said, rising suddenly to her feet. 'I knew there must be some such thing at work. I may be old, Professor, but my wits are still sharp enough. Allard will show you out.'

She rose and left him in the orangery.

Allard was leading him back through the silent house when Mrs Deveraux reappeared in coat and hat.

'There has been a change of plan,' she declared. 'I have decided to accompany you to Cambridge.'

'May I ask why?'

'I should like to meet my grandson in person. There is no time like the present.'

'His guardians would not agree. It would be a great shock to Oliver.'

Mrs Deveraux, clearly used to having her way, looked irritated. 'I mean the child no harm. I merely wish to meet him.'

'He cannot be interrupted without warning. It would be unsettling. He is not a specimen or some sort of curiosity to be taken up and set down on a whim.'

The old lady, who was now carrying a stick, tapped it once or twice in irritation on the patterned tiling of the floor. 'I intend to take the steps you suggest.'

He looked at her curiously. 'Which steps, precisely?'

'My son shall no longer have an allowance from the estate.'

'You will cut him off?'

'There is a property in Argentina. I shall make it a condition that he lives there. I shall see to it that my son does not ruin any more lives.'

Theo looked at the old lady standing fiercely upright in the hall. Her face was calm and determined, but she was trembling.

'If catching sight of Oliver from a distance would suffice, I think that could be arranged.'

'Today?'

'Yes. He has a swimming lesson.'

Chapter Twenty-Six

In Emmanuel College gardens, a small pavilion, fragrant with climbing roses and honeysuckle, offered a sheltered view of the swimming pool.

Theo settled Mrs Deveraux there in the shade. He had planned to leave, but within moments Will Halfpenny was sprinting over the grass and throwing himself into the pool, closely followed by Oliver. To his great surprise, Ida appeared too. She sat on the bench by the pool. She was to have a demonstration of Oliver's progress, it seemed.

'So this is the boy?' Mrs Deveraux asked. She peered through the rose entwined trellising. 'We are a long way away. I can barely see him.'

'This is Oliver.'

Obligingly, the boy climbed out of the pool and began to demonstrate his newly acquired diving skills, standing on the pool's edge with his hands held above his head each time before plunging in.

'Bravo!' Ida called, applauding from her bench.

'And this young woman? Who is she?'

Theo hesitated, suddenly wondering what he had got himself into by bringing Mrs Deveraux here. 'That is Ida Moss. Oliver's aunt.'

'Is it indeed?' The old lady peered at Ida. 'So this is your intended bride?'

'That is my private concern.'

She looked at him with bright eyes. 'The matter is confidential?'

'It is.'

The old lady cocked an eyebrow at this. She looked back at the pool.

'Oh, my grandson dives rather well, I believe. His father cannot swim at all. The water was always too cold, he said. I myself was once a strong swimmer, as it happens.'

From that distance, they could only see the boy when he climbed out onto the side of the pool. Once the diving part was over, he was less visible. Ida rose from the bench and began wandering the garden, pausing to take in the scent of a rose here and there.

'She dresses in a modest way, which is a good sign,' Mrs Deveraux remarked. 'And she has an appealing enough figure and good facial features…'

Theo, squirming and indignant at this cool assessment, did not know how to reply. He could only watch Ida himself, feeling a tug in his chest as, unaware of the scrutiny, she strolled the lawn in the sunshine.

'She seems a little sad. A little preoccupied, I'd say. She does not, to my eyes, have the look of a young woman who has been swept off her feet by love. But I am old. Perhaps I am mistaken.' Mrs Deveraux was enjoying herself. 'She has rather too many freckles for a perfect complexion…'

'Hush!' Theo said. 'She is looking this way.'

It was true. Ida had wandered from the poolside,

exploring the garden. She was less than thirty feet from the pavilion. As they looked on, she pulled something from her pocket. It was the letter. She unfolded it and scanned it briefly before putting it away again. Was that a shy smile? Did she press it for a mere second to her heart before it went back into her pocket? He wasn't sure.

Theo closed his eyes. What would Ida think if she found him spying? She would wonder who this lady was. She would expect him to introduce her! The last time he had failed to introduce someone, her feelings had been badly hurt, but if she found him there with Mrs Deveraux, of all the people in the world!

He stood and pressed himself into the shadows at the back corner of the pavilion.

'You hide from your fiancé. How very strange!' Mrs Deveraux remarked, rather enjoying the situation.

'Hush! I beg you!'

Nobody had hushed Antoinette Deveraux since she was a child. She turned and looked again at Ida, who was wandering back towards the pool. 'Those boots of hers have seen better days,' she remarked. 'It did not occur to me that they might be poor, but I suppose they are.'

Watt, in his corner, closed his eyes and took a deep breath, silently praying for patience.

'May I see their house? I should like to know my grandson's living conditions.'

'Absolutely not. I have explained.'

'I only wish to see it from the outside. From the cab window. There can be no harm in that. I am not a monster, Professor.'

'I can't take the cab down Cooper Street, Sir, that's too narrow. The old hoss can't turn hisself round with the cab, see? No room. Harrow street is close enough, it's only a short step. Will that do for you?'

'Yes, we can see from there. We're not leaving the cab. This lady only wants to look down Cooper Street.'

The cab driver made a face, but wasn't about to question the odd wishes of a paying customer. 'Just as you like,' he said.

When he stopped on the corner, Theo pointed out the house with the blue door and Mrs Devereaux put her head out of the window to get a better look. As she did, a lean, shabbily dressed man pushed past the cab and hurried by. Outside the Moss house, he paused and pulled a hammer from his jacket. Glancing rapidly up and down the street, he raised it an and smashed several small panes of glass in the front window. The sound of shattering echoed around the houses. Shouts of alarm came immediately from all sides. Heads were thrust out of front doors. Theo jumped from the cab and ran after the man, who had dropped his hammer and was hurrying away.

'Stop him!' He shouted. 'Stop that man! Someone stop him!'

A large man stepped out of one of the houses and joined the chase, close on Theo's heels. Further up the street, more doors opened, and a general outcry arose, as people who had heard or seen the attack joined in.

'Stop him!'

'He's smashed a window!'

'Stop that man!'

A few houses further down, a milkman with a barrow stepped forward and blocked the man's path. 'No, you don't!' he said, brandishing a large ladle.

It stopped the man long enough for Theo and the large neighbour to lay hands on the criminal. The larger man pushed him, panting, up against the wall of the house nearby. The man, thin and unshaven, cringed and looked about in panic.

'I never done nothing!' he said.

'You smashed that window!'

'I never!'

'A dozen people saw you do it. Call a constable, someone.'

'No!' the man cried. 'It wasn't my fault!'

'You did it. We all saw you,' Watt said. 'Why did you break that window?'

'I was sent to do it.'

'Sent? Who sent you?'

'I don't know his name. A man. A posh bloke in a big carriage give me five shillings to put a hammer through that front window. He give me the address and said to do it quick.'

'He's lying,' one of the neighbours said. Several others agreed.

'Alf's gone for the constable,' someone said.

'This man,' Theo said. 'Where was he?'

The offender shrugged. 'Waiting for someone on the Chesterton Road.'

'Waiting for who?'

'For his boy, he said.'

Watt turned and ran. He stopped at the cab and called to the driver to take Mrs Deveraux back to the station, then headed for the Chesterton Road.

Chapter Twenty-Seven

The running figure of the professor might have aroused more curiosity in the streets of Cambridge, if it hadn't been a hot enough afternoon to keep most people indoors in the shade. Those who were out were strolling by the river, where the air was cool, and bright handcarts sold cold drinks and ices.

Watt was red-faced and gasping by the time he reached Victoria Bridge. He peered in both directions, but his view was impeded by the many parasols of strolling ladies on both banks of the river. Beyond them, on the far side, a throng of carriages stopped and started on the road. There were cyclists and carts and carriages, pony traps and single riders, all enjoying the warm afternoon and the breeze along the Cam. That part of the river was used by narrowboats delivering fruit and vegetables from downriver farms to the water gates of the colleges. Two such vessels were side by side, the boatmen leaning on their brass rudder poles, talking, as they made their way back toward the lock.

Watt leaned, panting, on the bridge wall, peering in

both directions before he caught sight of the two figures he was seeking. They were strolling by the river hand-in-hand. Ida pointed out a swan family with seven cygnets to the boy, and the pair paused to watch the elegant parents lead their grey, fluffy offspring among the reeds. Theo's attention was caught by a carriage approaching them from behind. It was a grander, newer carriage than most, with glossier, larger horses. The driver, holding a long whip, seemed to pay no attention to the ambling riders and carts idling along, but came at speed. The sound made people stop and turn. A head leaned out of the window and shouted a command, urging the driver on. Watt recognised him. It was Devereaux.

Watt ran on. Swerving between couples and sidestepping children, he hurled himself in the direction of Ida and the child, but was still twenty feet away as the carriage drew alongside them. He saw the door open. Deveraux jumped out, ran to the boy, grabbed him by one arm and dragged Oliver kicking and struggling back across the pavement into the open door of the waiting carriage.

'Drive on!' Devereaux shouted, pushing the child inside and climbing up after him.

'Stop him! He is stealing the child! The boy! Stop him, someone!' Ida's frantic shouts alerted everyone by the river. She ran towards the moving carriage, reaching after Oliver, but Deveraux had already slammed the door.

'Drive on!' he shouted again.

People on all sides turned to see the disturbance.

The driver pulled past a row of idling cabs so closely that Ida was forced to step back, narrowly avoiding being crushed between the wheels. She waved her arms, calling for help from those about her, 'No! No! He is taking the child! Somebody stop him! He must be stopped!'

Gentlemen onlookers began to respond, running towards the carriage, but Watt reached it first. The shouts and general disturbance had frightened a horse which bucked and leapt across its path, forcing Deveraux's carriage to a shuddering halt. As it rocked on its springs, the door flew open and the small figure of Oliver hurled itself out. He fell to the road for a second, then scrambling dangerously among the shifting hooves of frightened horses, picked himself up and ran headlong across the pavement toward the river.

Shouting, Devereaux jumped out and followed.

The long grassy bank running down to the river was steep at this point. The boy, terrified, and wanting only to get away, tripped, fell and rolled down the grass, ending up on the river's walled edge. He looked back over his shoulder, saw Devereaux coming, and to the horror of the crowd, leapt into the water close to the advancing bows of one of the narrowboats. A woman in the crowd shrieked. Voices were raised from all sides, calling to the boatmen to stop their vessels from crushing the boy.

Watt, panting hard, now reached Deveraux on the grass bank. He laid hands on his arm. 'I am arresting you, Sir,' he said, 'for the…'

Devereaux hardly even looked at Watt before dealing him a fierce blow across the face with the handle of the riding crop he was carrying. The impact was powerful enough to send Watt flying backwards onto the grass. One part of his brain was strongly inclined to stay there on the cool sward, but it was swiftly overruled. The thought of Ida and all that this bully had done forced him to his feet, breathless and grass-stained.

Devereaux, by far the taller and stronger, thought he had dealt with the minor threat posed by this particular opponent and was looking away, searching for the boy, when Watt struck him back. It was an inefficient left-handed blow, hurting his own hand and striking his opponent's jaw at an unorthodox angle, but it was as hard as Watt could make it, and it took Devereaux by surprise. He staggered, clutching his face, letting out a brief howl of pain and fury.

'He's mine! The boy is mine! I must have my son!'

'The law forbids it, Sir!'

'The law will not stop me, and neither will you!'

'The law *will* stop you! You are a monstrous bully. You care nothing for the child.'

'What's it to you? Out of my way!'

Devereaux, trembling and red-faced, swiped again at Watt with his whip, but it was an ill-judged lunge, and missed. Watt, remembering some of the advice he had been given, stepped sharply in and aimed the hardest punch he could muster at the end of the bigger man's nose.

Devereaux roared and staggered back, clutching at this face before his knees gave way, and he fell forward, howling and bleeding.

Bystanders pressed forward.

'This man,' Watt declared to them, 'is attempting to kidnap the boy who has just thrown himself into the river. He must be detained.'

'A police officer is on the way!' one man called. He joined two others who held Deveraux down as a policeman struggled through the crowd.

Watt stumbled to the river. The whip's impact on his face made his eyes water so badly he could barely see. Oliver was out of sight. The boy must have swum between the heavy barges, or been crushed, or pulled under. To the shock of everyone on the river bank Watt threw himself untidily in. It certainly couldn't be called a dive.

When he surfaced, all Watt could see was the hulking prow of a green narrowboat rising steeply in front of him on one side, and the dank green brickwork of the riverbank on the other. The boy must be between, or worse still, under the boats. He must find him.

He struck out using a swimming stroke Will Halfpenny would not have recognised and managed to round the towering bows of the first boat. In the long watery canyon between the two narrowboats, he found Oliver treading water. Some of the fear left Oliver's face when he saw Watt. 'He tried to take me, but I ran away, Sir,' the boy said, gasping.

'I saw it,' Watt told him. 'He cannot take you. You are safe, Oliver. There is a policeman to stop him now.' He tried to say more, but all his efforts had to go into keeping his head, or at least his nose, out of the water. He had already swallowed many mouthfuls of the foul-smelling stuff that wanted to pull him down.

On either side, the black painted sides of the narrowboats continued to slide past. It was oddly quiet and shadowy down there in the water. It might almost have been peaceful, except that every ounce of Watt's effort had to go into keeping his head from going under. He tried to appear calm and encouraging to Oliver, but secretly suspected he himself would soon be joining the whiskery fish that lived at the bottom of the Cam. On the whole, he thought, saving the boy is a cause worth dying for, but there was so much more I wanted to tell Ida.

'If you reach down, I think your feet might reach the bottom, Sir,' Oliver said.

With a struggle, Watt brought his feet down, and yes, they touched the mud first, and then the slippery stonework built into the bed of the river. He was not going to drown, after all.

As one boatman held the two vessels apart with his bargepole, the other walked along the side and leaned down, reaching a boathook to hook the boy by the waistband. 'I got you, boy,' he told him. 'Out you come.'

A moment later, a circular cork life preserver landed in the water beside Watt, who grabbed it, and was relieved to find that it had the power to keep afloat even someone as determined to sink as he was. It had a rope attached to it, and he was soon hauled to the bank, where many hands reached down to pull him onto the sunny grass bank beside the boy.

They sat, side by side, catching their breath and saw two policemen, one on each side, march Deveraux off towards a blue police carriage that had pulled out of the traffic on the other side of the river.

As they watched, the figure of a well-dressed lady appeared through the crowd and before anyone could prevent her, dealt the prisoner several forceful blows over the head with her parasol.

'Will he go to prison?' Oliver asked.

'I expect so.'

'Will he stay there forever?'

'Not forever, but he will not bother you or your Aunt Ida for a good long time.'

'That lady just hit him!'

'That is your grandmother,' Theo said.

A generous passer-by handed Oliver an ice cream.

Ida ran to them. She hugged the dripping boy, burying sobs of relief in his wet hair.

'The police took him away, Ida,' he told her, 'and somebody gave me an ice cream!' He licked it in celebration.

'Theo?'

He did not move. He lay on his back in the warmth of the sunshine with his eyes closed and thought how pleasant his own name sounded when she said it.

She put a hand on his chest. Still, he did not move, but she could feel a heart, could feel it jump beneath her palm. She leaned near to check his breath against her cheek. He would not die, surely? Not now. His mouth moved and breathed. She turned her face. Her lips brushed his.

His hand tightened on her arm.

Chapter Twenty-Eight

King Henry VIII glared and pursed his lips in his usual challenge across the Trinity College dining room. Was the wine that evening particularly fine, Watt wondered, or was that watery feeling in his stomach due to something else?

'You are quite the hero, Watt, I believe,' the Bursar remarked. He was a long-faced man whose expression usually suggested he had eaten something unpleasant, although the guinea fowl on his plate was well up to the usual standard.

'You were in the evening papers, or so I'm told,' the Master said. He preferred to give the impression that he never read newspapers himself. 'Quite the centre of attention.'

A silence of some minutes passed. Watt looked uncertainly at his dinner while the college officials who had invited him ate on.

'One of the main considerations, as far as we are concerned,' the Master continued, 'is continuity and dependability. We hope—we always hope—that a Senior

Tutor will see out several generations of undergraduates. The post is a cornerstone of the College, as you know. And I for one am delighted that… ' he broke off in surprise as Watt stood suddenly and left with the briefest apology.

The next time he woke, Theo was in his boyhood bed in Grange Road. The wallpaper was familiar, as was the iron bedstead, the library of favourite childhood books and the row of medicine bottles on the bedside table.

'Oh there, you're awake, Master Theo. Just in time for your tea.' It was Hanks.

'Hanks, why am I here?' he asked.

'Oh, this and that,' she said. 'A touch of the old trouble—your chest—and then, well, the doctor said it was probably something from the river water. You've been poorly. It was quite a do, but you're looking better now that the fever's gone. The tea will do you a power of good. Drink it up.'

'How long has it been?'

'The best part of a fortnight, I'd say.'

'*Two weeks?*'

'All sorts of people were asking after you and sending notes. You were in the college sick bay at first, but then we brought you here. Your mother will tell you about it. She'll be up in a minute.'

Mrs Professor Watt, when she appeared, looked livelier and more energetic than Theo remembered.

'So glad you're feeling better, Theo,' she told him, rearranging his pillows. 'You have been quite unwell.'

He sat up, remembering. 'We had a falling out, I think.'

His mother, sitting on the bedside chair, looked slightly pained. 'We did, but that has all blown over now.'

'Has it?'

'Yes, it has. We disagreed over Miss Moss. Miss Moss is no longer a subject of disagreement.'

A look of alarm passed over Theo's face. 'What makes you say that? Has something happened to her?'

'No, no.' His mother dismissed his anxieties with a brisk shake of her head. 'She is perfectly well. I saw her yesterday, as a matter of fact.'

'You saw her?'

'I visited her at the hat shop.'

'She helped you select a new hat?'

'No purchase was made. I went to speak to her.' Theo could only look bewildered. 'I wanted to talk things over. We went to the Copper Kettle. They serve excellent Viennese pastries.' His mother straightened her back and adjusted the lace on her bodice. 'If she is to be my daughter-in-law, I felt the least I could do was… '

'You have changed your mind?'

This was a step further than Mrs Watt was prepared to go. 'Shall we say I have revised my view.'

'Why?'

His mother sighed and rolled her eyes. 'Well, if you must know, it was Hanks. A conversation with Hanks.'

'Hanks the maid?'

'She came to me, after you and I had fallen out, and she made a speech. She told me she was handing in her notice because I was being ridiculous. I was standing in the way of your happiness.'

'Good heavens!'

'I was outraged, naturally I was. The impertinence! The effrontery! A maid speaking to her mistress in such a way! I sent her away to pack her bags. But, frankly, her words had the ring of honest truth. I tried, but I could not dismiss what she had said. I waited a few days and then realised I could not dismiss Hanks either. What would I do without her? We have lived alongside each other since we were young women. And then you collapsed at the dinner, and of course she instantly returned to help nurse you. She truly believes her beef broth is the only reason you are still living. And then Mr Moss and Oliver knocked on the door and asked after you. They were worried. So we met, and, well, dear, Oliver is such a charming boy. He counted seventeen frogs in the pond yesterday.'

'He visits often?'

'I refused them entry at first, but they walked here every day to ask after you. Right across town. Every day. And in the hottest weather. Hanks insisted on offering them refreshments. So, well, we have come to know one another a little. Mr Moss and I discussed the matter of your courtship of Ida…'

'Oh, did you really?'

'… yes, and we are agreed that it is acceptable to us both.'

Theo put his hands to his head in wonder.

'There is another thing, Theodore. I am not so cold-hearted that I could watch a family thrown out of their home without offering help. I have invited them to live here. Mr Moss insists on paying rent. There is plenty of room.'

There was a pause of several minutes while Theo's convalescent brain attempted to take all this in. 'You no longer fear scandal? The same family was tainted forever last time we discussed this. Any connection risked ruining our reputation. *Polluting* was the word you used, I think.'

'As I said, I have revised my view of the matter,' his mother said with dignity. She stood and took an empty glass from his nightstand. 'Besides, dear, this is Cambridge. We have a neighbour who makes bombs on one side of us, and another who takes cold water baths in his garden on the other. We have our own way of doing things here.'

Theo smiled and fell back on the pillows. 'Mother, I hardly know what to say.'

She patted her son's hand where it lay on the bedcovers.

'The Senior Tutorship was offered to Wisley, Theo. A very poor choice, in my opinion. A very dull choice. I hope you are not too disappointed.'

'I am not disappointed in the least. Are you disappointed, Mother?'

'I have hardly given it a thought. I've been too busy. I must speak to Hanks about supper now. The household is a lot busier than it used to be. I have to keep my wits about me. Doctor Mead says you can get up as soon as you're strong enough, but you are not to work for at least two weeks. He recommended a holiday. Oh, and you have a letter from Ida.'

She took an envelope from her pocket and handed it to him before bustling away.

Dear Theo,

My father believes that anyone can do anything, as long as they find the right library books. I agree.

It has not been books that have illuminated my life lately, but Dr Solomons' ancient parchments. The pile I work on contains fragments of advice to the living from those approaching death. I am not familiar with the language of these eight hundred-year-old messages, but I noticed the same pattern of writing—the same word or phrase—occurring repeatedly. When Dr Solomons saw it, he told me the word was 'love'.

What people in their last moments want successive generations to know is nearly always something about love. Some name the people they love or have loved in the past. They thank them. They say goodbye.

Some express regret because they loved the wrong person, or failed to love the right one.

A surprisingly large majority of these writers, however, choose to leave the same piece of advice. It is expressed in different forms, but again and again it amounts to this: have the courage not to look away, if love shines its light into your heart.

You did not look away; you swam towards it.

I am not brave enough to say more, Theo, not yet.

I believe you still owe me a farthing. When you are well, and ready to repay it, you can find me at the hat shop or the library. If you do not choose to repay it, I utterly forgive the debt, and hope we will always remain friends.

Sincerely,
Ida Moss (Miss)

Chapter Twenty-Nine

Will Halfpenny was at dinner on the first night Theo returned to college.

'I heard you'd recovered, old man! Good to see you well,' he said, taking a seat on his right.

'You seem cheerful, Halfpenny. Is this a sign that have you prevailed with Gwendolyn's father?'

'I have indeed. We are engaged to be married in two weeks' time.' Halfpenny beamed a broad grin out across the mostly empty dining hall.

'That is magnificent news, Halfpenny. Congratulations!'

'Thank you. It was far from easy. The old man took a lot of persuading. At one moment he wanted us to wait *five years*, but the females all took my side and no man could withstand the collective force of the females of the Hurst family!'

'So you will be married before the family leaves for Heidelberg?'

'We shall. I have found us pleasant rooms in Alpha Road to come back to after we honeymoon in Wales. We shall not be wealthy, but Gwendolyn plans to continue her school teaching.'

A college servant reached in and placed a plate of trout in aspic before each of them.

'I must enjoy this fine dining while I can. Dinners like this will not be within my budget as a newlywed. Dare I ask about you and Ida?'

'She is avoiding me, I think.'

'Oh dear. A falling out?'

'No, no. Matters between us are simply unsettled. I have yet to take decisive action.'

They both ate a few forkfuls of the trout.

'You hesitate?' Halfpenny asked.

'No. I only take my time to choose the right moment.'

'That is not good!'

Another voice interrupted from Theo's left. It was Dr Brünerhof at full volume.

'You should not—oh, what is the word? You should not *prevaricate*, Watt. Get the job done! A beautiful lady should never be kept waiting. I am right, yes?'

'Dr Brünerhof *is* right,' Halfpenny said.

'I was merely choosing the location—the setting, as it were—for the proposal.'

Brünerhof sighed and shook his head.

'A punt is good,' Halfpenny said. 'The long trip to Grantchester is especially conducive.'

'Wherever it is to be, make it *soon*!' the German said.

'I'm not sure I can use a punting pole, though,' Watt said.

'Have you punted before?'

'Yes, as an undergraduate.'

'Well, then you can still punt. It is like riding a bicycle. One never forgets.'

Watt did not like to tell them he did not ride a bicycle either.

He looked up and caught the small but piercing eye of the portrait of Henry VIII. It seemed to be sneering at him.

'A punt it is,' he said.

'That cat has unwound a whole spool of my best lace!' Christabel said, flourishing the evidence. 'He has dragged it across the floor. He has ripped it and chewed it. Five shillings, that lace cost! I shall have to have strong words with Miss Peach about this.'

'Miss Peach won't hear a word against Blossom.'

'We'll see about that! What are you writing? You've been there scribbling away for an hour.'

Lucia sighed. 'My report for Mr Dixon. The one whose fiancée went somewhere every Thursday, remember?'

'Where did she go? Last I heard, you were about to follow her.'

'Well, that's just it. I did follow her, and she went to a meeting hall in Chesterton.'

'So she was at a church meeting? Not much he could object to there.'

'I told him where she was going, but that was not enough. He wanted me to go in. So the following week, I did.'

'And?'

'It was a spiritualist meeting. With a medium. A funny little woman with an eye patch. She sort of lolled about in a trance and spoke to people in a strange voice. Anyway, the fiancée just sat and listened that first week, so that was all I could report. He wanted me to keep going until she spoke or did something, so he could know what she was doing. Why she was going there. I've been three times now, but finally last night…'

The shop doorbell rang, and both sisters jumped to attention, but turning, they saw it was only Ida.

'Did I surprise you?' She came in carrying a basket.

'I do hope you have hummingbirds,' Christabel hurried over. 'At least five ladies are waiting for hummingbirds.'

'I have hummingbirds in six different variations.' Ida unwrapped a tissue parcel on the counter.

'They are delightful!'

Lucia left her writing and came to admire.

'Isn't one for my former client, the mother of the professor?'

'Yes, this one, with the longer tail, as she requested. I apologise for keeping her waiting.'

'She has not been here to ask, so I imagine she is not too impatient.'

'Her son has been ill,' Ida said.

The sisters looked at her curiously.

'But he is quite recovered now.'

Lucia's next question was interrupted by the doorbell ringing again. Professor Watt nodded politely as he entered.

'Ah, Professor, we were just discussing your mother's hat. She has asked you to collect it for her, perhaps?' Christabel said.

'Her hat?' He seemed confused by this. 'No. I came to settle a debt with Miss Moss, as a matter of fact.'

He produced a farthing from his pocket and, bowing, presented it with ceremony to Ida, who received it with a smile.

'Perhaps you would care to join me for a picnic on the river, Ida?'

The Venables sisters looked on with shameless curiosity.

'That would be delightful. When do you suggest?'

'I suggest now.'

'Immediately?'

'Unless you have urgent hat business, that is.'

'No, I have completed my hat business, as you put it.'

'Good, then we leave immediately. All arrangements are made.'

The professor held open the door. The bell rang again, and the pair left.

'Good heavens! What was that?'

'A romantic gesture followed by a significant invitation, unless I am much mistaken,' Lucia said.

'The unmarriageable professor appears to be in pursuit of our little Ida Moss. How did that come about?'

'It must've been Cupid. It certainly wasn't me,' her sister said.

They both looked out of the window after the couple.

'He wasn't a warthog, after all.'

'No. But I was telling you about my client at the spiritualist meeting.'

'Ah yes. So you went last night?'

'Yes. And she did speak this time. She sat at the front and asked if the medium could make contact with anyone called Vincent.'

'And who was Vincent?'

'Turns out Vincent was her late fiancé. She wanted to ask him what he thought about Mr Dixon.'

'Somehow I imagine Vincent would not care for Mr Dixon.'

'You're right. Vincent said Mr Dixon was an unpleasant

character who would make her unhappy. He told her to have nothing to do with Mr Dixon.'

'That was quite predictable, I suppose. And how did she take this advice from her dead fiancé?'

'She took it calmly, but I definitely had the feeling that she no longer planned to marry Mr Dixon. But the thing is…'

'Yes?'

'The medium knew her. She had asked the same question before.'

'About another fiancé?'

'About two others.'

'So the ghostly Vincent just keeps warning her off her admirers. Exerting his competitive influence from beyond the grave.'

'So it would seem. You can see why this report is taking me some time to write.'

'I can, yes.'

'How can I break it to him that he has failed the dead fiancé test?'

'Rather you than me,' Christabel said, then leapt suddenly up and hurried out of the shop. 'I've just seen that cat sneak into the store room again!'

Chapter Thirty

The punt was moored among the trailing branches of a weeping willow right at the end of the college gardens. A large picnic hamper and a checked rug were already on board.

Watt helped Ida in and sat opposite. They smiled at one another.

'Shall I help to cast off?' Ida asked, indicating the rope that tied them to a peg in the bank.

'I thought we might stay here,' Theo told her. He gestured over the manicured lawns towards the ancient honey-coloured walls of the great college. 'I chose this spot as the most conspicuous I could think of.'

'The most public?'

'Yes.'

'May I ask why you want us to eat our picnic in full view of the whole of Trinity College?'

'For two reasons,' he said. 'Firstly, because I wish everyone in Trinity College—everyone in the world, in fact, but I could not arrange that—to see us in company with one another.'

'Is this a very cautious form of chaperoning?' she suggested. 'The whole college protects our virtue at once?'

'No! It is a declaration. The loudest I can manage, of the pride I feel at being in your company, Ida Moss. I want everyone who looks at us to know who you are and how honoured I am to be here with you. No more hiding for you.'

'Oh, that's enough of that!'

'I mean it sincerely. I shall never hide you, or play down your identity, Ida.'

She looked at him squarely, guarded.

'You have not done, nor has anyone in your family done anything to be ashamed of. I shall never shame you, and I shall take on anyone else who does.'

'Thank you,' Ida said.

A duck paddled by. It eyed the picnic basket. She watched it pass.

'But, you said there were two reasons to remain moored here. What is the other?'

'This second reason is not as noble as the first. The fact is, I am not sure I can punt. I thought it might be wiser to… well, just to stay here.'

'Oh, come now!' she said.

'Come now?'

'You can do it! *We* can do it. We can work out some way of moving this boat! A picnic in a punt is a delightful thing, but even more so after an outing along the river, surely? Incidentally, this is a very large picnic basket. Are we expecting half a dozen guests?'

'Hanks has firm ideas about what constitutes a proper

picnic. A whole chicken is involved, and at least one game pie. Not to mention several bottles of champagne.'

They both looked at the hamper and laughed.

They untied the rope and loosened the punt pole from the riverbed. Theo stood a little gingerly at the punting end of the boat and pushed. The punt slid into the stream.

The course they took to Grantchester that day was not without incident. There were unsteady moments, and they lost the pole once, but soon retrieved it. They hit the bank near Darwin College and struck another punt a glancing blow near the Meadows, but escaped all harm, except for a few rivery splashes.

'You will marry me, Ida, won't you?' Theo asked, once they had moored at Grantchester beneath one of the great willows. He threw himself to his knees in the bottom of the boat, despite an inch or two of bilge water.

'Theo,' she said, 'you will rock the boat!'

'Say yes, Ida, and save us both.'

'But what of Oliver? What of my father?'

'If you will have me, Ida, you shall keep them close. I promise.'

He reached into his pocket, causing another tilt of the boat, and placed a small wooden object in her hand. It was a ring.

'Carved from another acorn,' he said. 'It can be replaced by something grander at a later date, if you prefer.'

'I prefer this one.'

'Marry me, Ida. Please.' He put the ring on her finger. The boat tilted back the other way, small waves splashing on either side.

'Yes!'

'Do you mean it?'

'Yes! I will marry you. Sit, Theo, you'll have us over!'

'Kiss me first!'
'We will both end up in the river!'
'I don't care! Kiss me, Ida!'

The punt tilted this way and that, but ballasted by the picnic hamper, it steadied, and the minnows in the dappled shade of the trees swam undisturbed upriver.

Next in The Moth Agency Romances

vinci-books.com/missmarshall

In Victorian Cambridge, can a gifted mathematician and a disgraced musician find love against all odds?

When Grace Marshall's father dies suddenly, marriage seems her only hope for security. Enter Daniel Hollingdale, a disgraced musician who needs Grace's tutoring to prove he's capable of serious study. Amidst scandal and romance, Grace and Daniel must navigate societal expectations and their own desires…

Turn the page for a free preview…

A Match for Miss Marshall: Chapter One

'I'm beginning to wonder whether Mr Murphy actually exists,' Christabel Venables remarked, over supper in the attic sitting room in Paradise Place.

The weather in Cambridge was unsteady that May of 1896; one moment high blue skies and warm sunshine, the next, a chill in the air and a downpour of rain. Both sisters were wrapped in woollen shawls that evening as banks of menacing grey cloud churned outside the skylight.

'You surely don't think Miss Peach would mislead us deliberately?' Lucia said.

Christabel raised an eyebrow. 'Is it really true that she can't climb the stairs? She seems nimble enough in other ways.' She paused to examine the food on her plate. 'Lucia, this is the thinnest slice of ham I have ever seen. You could read a letter through it.'

Her sister looked down at her own meal, which consisted, like Christabel's, of a pale sliver of ham, a small tomato and half the heel of a loaf. 'I only had sixpence left, but there are a few cherries.'

Christabel made a face. 'The last cherries from the market were soft.'

'These are better. They're still the market leftovers, but I got there earlier,' her sister said.

Christabel sighed and shook her head. 'I'm hoping several of my ladies will settle their accounts soon. There's quite a sum outstanding. Mrs Professor Perks, for example, has had three summer straws on account. Rather fine they were too, though I say so myself. Especially the navy one with the red and white ribbons.'

'You were saying about Mr Murphy,' Lucia reminded her.

'I begin to suspect Miss Peach of making him up.'

'Surely not. He is her builder.'

'Well, so she says, but we have never seen him.'

Both sisters sipped their tea and cast their minds back to the conversation they had had with their landlady when last the roof leaked. Carrying a bucket, Christabel had tackled her in the shared basement kitchen.

'Miss Peach, this bucket, that I have carried from our bedroom, is almost a quarter full of water that came through our leaking roof. Look! It dripped all night long.'

'Oh dear no, I don't think that can be so,' said Miss Peach. Their landlady was small and elderly, but sharp featured, with bright, darting eyes behind her silvery spectacles. Her large ginger cat, Blossom, was sitting on the kitchen table, which was forbidden. 'No, no, Mr Murphy assured me only last year that the roof was in perfect order.'

'Mr Murphy?' Christabel asked.

'My builder. One of Cambridge's premier builders. A craftsman through and through. Highly skilled. Absolutely reliable. Mr Murphy is very well known in the city.'

'Even so,' Christabel said, 'all this rainwater came through our ceiling last night.' She held up the bucket before carrying it to the sink and pouring the contents away.

'I can't imagine how that could have happened,' said Miss Peach. 'Mr Murphy is very reliable, as a rule.'

'There is a hole, Miss Peach. That is the only explanation,' Lucia said.

Their landlady swatted that idea aside with a lace-gloved hand.

Blossom looked on, moving his yellow eyes from one to the other as if memorising the conversation for future reference.

'Where could the rainwater have come from, in that case?' Christabel asked.

'Well,' said Miss Peach, looking away, 'water finds its way into buckets, you know.' Both sisters looked at her in disbelief. 'I mean to say that it is easy to mistake water that one finds in a bucket for rainwater,' Miss Peach continued. 'And then to imagine that it has come in through the roof, when in fact it is …' Lucia and Christabel looked intently at their landlady, wondering what she would say next. ' … in fact it is merely dew, or condensation.'

The sisters were temporarily rendered speechless. Blossom jumped off the table as if he, for one, had heard quite enough about leaky roofs.

'What we fear, Miss Peach,' Lucia said, 'is that if there is another night of hard rain, the dew or condensation you mention might bring down our ceiling as well as overflowing our bucket. I'm sure you would not want that to happen.'

'I shall ask Mr Murphy to look in at his earliest convenience,' said Miss Peach, 'but he is a busy man.'

With that, she had followed the cat out of the kitchen and into her private rooms.

Three weeks and two rainstorms later, there was still no sign of Mr Murphy. Buckets were emptied; leaking roofs were mentioned, but finding she was unable to climb the stairs to the attic bedroom to see for herself, Miss Peach still tended to favour the dew or condensation theory.

A Match for Miss Marshall: Chapter Two

The following morning was bright. New College was looking handsome with its ancient stonework bathed in sunlight and wisteria trailing a frothy haze of purple flowers along the cloisters. The young man who knocked at the door of the Master's Lodge seemed taken aback when Grace answered.

'I was hoping to see Miss Marshall,' he said.

'Yes?' She peered around the door, not opening it completely to the stranger.

'I believe it is Miss Grace Marshall that I should speak to,' he repeated, smiling.

'I am she.'

He took a step back, accidentally treading into a flower bed, and almost lost his balance. 'Excuse me, but I was expecting someone… rather different,' he said.

Grace waited. She was wearing an old apron and had a duster tied around her hair. She had been packing.

The young man regained his footing and offered his

most charming smile. 'I'm told you offer tuition. I need a little practice before I sit an examination.'

Grace blinked at him, still not opening the door. 'Examination?' she said. 'The examinations are over.'

The young man's smile faded. 'I am a special case.'

Grace scrutinised the young man standing on her doorstep. He was tall and sandy-haired, with a loose fringe falling over one eye. His academic gown fluttered around him. Beneath it, he wore a dark suit and a foppishly colourful waistcoat, giving him a Bohemian look. He was the kind of figure her father would have scorned on sight as a time-waster, someone whose attention was more likely directed at his choice of cravat than his books.

'And what kind of tuition are you seeking, exactly, Mister…?'

'Hollingdale. Daniel Hollingdale.'

They were still speaking around the edge of the door.

'What is it that you wish to study, Mr. Hollingdale?'

'Mathematics,' he said simply.

'Well, obviously mathematics, but which branch? Algebra? Trigonometry? Calculus?'

'Elementary mathematics, if you please. I can't make head or tail of it,' he smiled broadly and shrugged.

Grace looked at him in some confusion. 'But you have attended lectures and so forth?'

'Not in mathematics. I study music,' he smiled expectantly, then added, 'strictly speaking.'

James, one of the handymen, whistled a tune from the kitchen, then passed behind Grace in the hallway carrying a pot of paint.

'I am about to move house. I cannot teach anyone at present,' she said, and closed the door.

A Match for Miss Marshall: Chapter Three

'Marriage would be the obvious solution,' the Bursar remarked. He looked out of his office window towards the Master's Lodge. Miss Froment followed his gaze. Through a window they could just make out the figure of Grace Marshall bent over a desk.

The Bursar shrugged and picked up his pen. 'What about that visiting Swede? Or the mathematician who worked with her father - what was his name?'

'Dr Hillyer? He left for Switzerland.'

'Only temporarily. You have told her she must vacate soon, I trust?'

Miss Froment nodded.

'We have no obligation to house her. There is nowhere in the least suitable. We are pressed for accommodation, as you know. The new Master and his family move in at the end of the month.'

The Bursar considered the matter at an end. Miss Froment, who had worked with him for more than twenty years, was not so easily dismissed.

'Isn't there a small gardener's cottage in the grounds of Abercrombie House?' She asked this as if it were a casual enquiry.

'I don't recall one. If there is, it has not been inhabited in my time.'

'But if it could be sufficiently repaired?'

'There is no budget for rebuilding.'

'Perhaps none will be needed. If it required only cleaning and a little decoration?'

The Bursar looked unenthusiastic but did not absolutely refuse. His Head of Housekeeping pressed her advantage. 'I have your permission to inspect the cottage and use the staff to carry out minor repairs?'

'As long as she is out of the Master's Lodge by the end of the month. But it cannot be a long-term arrangement. Grace Marshall, in her own right, no longer has any role at the College. She will have to fend for herself. Or marry, as I said.'

Miss Froment slipped out of the door.

Grab your copy…
vinci-books.com/missmarshall

Afterword

There really was a scandalous divorce case in the 1880s like the one I used in this story. The Langworthy case ran for months in the London Newspapers in 1887. A fascinated public followed every twist and turn of the story of a young woman deceived into false marriage by the very rich Edward Langworthy who then abandoned and repudiated her when she fell pregnant. After I read about it, I was left wondering how the remaining family members in such a case could possibly make a life for themselves. Out of that came the fictional character of Ida, the younger sister.

The rescue of the chub happened in real life too. Olms are real, they do live in the mud of dark caves and don't have any eyes, but whether they swim towards a bright light I can't be sure. I might have made that part up...

Lucy Greenhill

Cambridge
April 2023

About the Author

Lucy Greenhill loves to write stories whose starting point is a real incident or place and can often be found searching archives and libraries.

The inspiration for *An Utterly Unsuitable Lady* was the notorious case in the 1860s of a rich man who fooled an innocent young woman into a fraudulent marriage before abandoning her without a penny. Could a happy life be salvaged from such wreckage?

The Moth Agency Romances introduce Lucia and Christabel Venables, an independently-minded pair of sisters living in Victorian Cambridge. Christabel runs a hat shop and Lucia is proprietor of the agency which introduces ladies and gentlemen pursuing romance and generally looks into Matters Of The Heart. There are plenty more Moth Agency Romances to come.

Lucy also writes Edwardian mysteries under the pen name of Fran Smith. She lives with her husband, dog and chickens on the edge of the fens near Cambridge, England.

www.ingramcontent.com/pod-product-compliance
Ingram Content Group UK Ltd.
Pitfield, Milton Keynes, MK11 3LW, UK
UKHW040252230426
470297UK00004B/112